BOURBON · PENN ·

18

July 2019

Bourbon Penn Issue 18
July 2019

Copyright © 2019 by Cognitive Wave, Inc.

www.bourbonpenn.com
Myrtle Beach, SC

Editor:
Erik Secker

Copy Editing:
J. Scott Wilson

Cover Art:
On Earth As It Is In Heaven
copyright © by Horacio Quiroz

CONTENTS

MY NAME IS ELLIE

■

Sam Rebelein

My name is Ellie, and I like figurines made of ceramic.

Not the little angels or the ones based on paintings, but the ones that are just little people.

Which I know is not what most 10-year-olds are into, but I like them.

Which is something my mom says I picked up from my grandma.

Which is my mom's mom.

Which is funny because I also got my name from my grandma, whose name was Ellen.

Which, for a while, was pretty much the only thing I knew about my grandma, who died before I was born.

Which my dad once said, at a party when he was very drunk, is a good thing.

Which is because she scared him.

Which my mom told me is only because my dad is intimidated by women who know things he doesn't.

Which she said is all women.

Which my dad said isn't true and she knows it, that's not why he was afraid of her.

To which my mom said, "Shut up or I'll dip you in glaze and pose you myself."

Which I didn't really understand.

"Intimidated" isn't really a word I understand either.

Anyway.

The only other thing I know about my grandma is that she lived in a large lonely house in the middle of the woods.

Which my mom says smelled very nice when it rained.

Which she says was one of her favorite things about living in that house when she was my age.

Which always makes me wish I'd gotten to meet my grandma, and see her house.

Which is gone now.

Which is sad, because my mom says it was beautiful and had lots of stained glass and "gables".

Which sounds fancy even though I don't know what a gable is.

My mom says that the house was surrounded by pine trees, and that the air was always misty so you couldn't see the tops of the trees, and that the house was so high up in the hills that when you couldn't see the tops of the trees, it felt like you couldn't see the very top of the world itself.

Which my dad says is horseshit.

Which my mom says is a bad word, and whenever he says it, she makes him put a dollar in a jar on our counter.

Which my dad always does without grumbling.

Which my mom says is because he's actually very nice (and he is!); he just gets scared when she talks about my grandma, that's all.

Which Mom says is also why Dad won't go in my bedroom at night, and why he sometimes won't even go in there by himself during the day.

Which can be annoying sometimes, if she asks him to go in there to get my laundry, to help her with the chores, or something.

But which she also understands, because of all the ceramic figurines in my room.

Which he says he's never liked, ever since he met my grandma.

Which my mom says was in college, during a winter break.

Which was about a year after they'd started going out.

Which I think is gross to think about—my parents going out.

Anyway.

My mom says that my dad really liked Grandma's house, too, and that he even liked all the figurines at first.

Which was good, because Grandma Ellen had lots of them on the shelves all around her house.

My dad says there were hundreds. All standing around in suits and fine dresses, waving to each other or playing games or doing other simple poses. All over the house. On shelves, in cabinets, on the mantel, on tables, on the stairs, and just standing on the floor. At Christmastime, they hid three Christmas figurines in the house, all wearing Santa suits, and whoever found them got a candy cane.

Which my grandpa never approved of, because he thought candy was the devil, but which is one reason why my mom says I would have liked Grandma Ellen's house.

My mom says I also would have liked the house because everything was a dark, rich wood, and all the ceilings were carved into arches, and all the rooms echoed if you yelled, and you could stand in one corner and whisper to someone in another corner and they'd whisper back, and the wallpaper was very pretty, and there was a library filled with books (which sounds like heaven to me), and because there were people who lived inside of the walls.

Which my mom says she told my dad about before he visited for the first time.

Which she says she was really nervous about—even more than him meeting her parents.

Which she says is because she thought he might think she was crazy.

Which, my dad says, he did.

At first.

My dad says he thought the house was too big. He hated all the open space. He didn't like how lonely it was. And he says the "altitude" (which means it's very high up, which I said already) messed with his head and made him dizzy whenever he climbed the stairs. He didn't like looking out the windows at the trees and not knowing where the trees ended. He says the mist made him nervous.

Which my mom says is only because he doesn't have a sense of mystery.

Which I understand, because my dad is always the one who plans everything and keeps track of stuff.

Which my mom calls "being grounded".

Which she likes about him.

But which she also says can be a bad thing, because it means you're not open to new and weird stuff.

Which is why my dad didn't believe her about the people in the walls, and why he still doesn't like all my figurines. He's just not open.

To which my dad says, "That's definitely a way to put it."

Which he says without looking at Mom or me.

My dad says he figured my mom was just hearing mice in the walls, or some other critters. He says she must have been scared sleeping as a little girl in a big lonely house in the middle of the woods.

Which my mom says is wrong because the woods never bothered her, and the sounds she heard were definitely people sounds.

Which she says included things like laughter, utensils clicking against plates, bootsteps, teeth-brushing, and whispers.

Which she says would only happen at night, and only after everyone else was asleep.

That's when she'd hear them wake up.

Which she says sounded mostly normal—like people yawning and shuffling around and making coffee and making that sleepy murmuring you hear people do in bed just after they wake up—except smaller.

Which she says is because *they* were much smaller—only about a foot tall.

Which meant their days were shorter.

Which she says always started with them making tea.

Which she always thought was terrible because she could hear the kettle on the stove whistling, shrill and loud, through the wall.

Which was then followed by the sounds of the people going about their day.

Which included them reading the paper, playing games with each other, two meals, and a snack right before dawn, when they would go to sleep.

Which my mom says she heard every single night, for years, ever since she was a very little girl.

My dad says she told him this, and he thought she was kidding.

But then, he says, he heard it, too.

The first night he stayed at my grandma's, my mom fell asleep right away (forgetting about the people in the walls, she was so used to it), and my dad was left alone to listen to their sounds all night long, scared stiff.

He heard them make tea.

He heard them read the paper.

He heard them play chess.

He heard them laughing.

He heard them dancing.

And then, at dawn, he heard them pick one of their people and tear them apart limb by limb with their bare hands.

Which he's only told me once or twice, and both times it made his hands shake.

He says he could hear all of it.

He says he *knows* it happened because he could hear, through the wall over the bed, the skin bursting and the joints ripping and the screams of the one chosen and the chant of the ones doing the killing.

Which went, "This is our choice. This is our choice. This is our choice."

Which my dad says he could hear all over the wall.

Which he says must have been filled with hundreds, maybe thousands of people.

"This is our choice. This is our choice. This is our choice."

Which they said over and over as they did the "butchering".

Which my dad says is the only word for it.

Which he says was then followed by all the people in the walls, very formally, saying good night to one another.

Which was followed by silence, as dawn slid through the window.

In the morning, Grandma Ellen smiled at him and asked him if he heard the people in the walls.

Which my mom says she'd forgotten about, she'd been so tired.

Which she said she was sorry about, because she'd meant to stay up with him so he wasn't scared.

My dad said he *did* hear, and did they know the people in the walls killed each other?

My dad says that this was the worst part because Mom and Grandma Ellen just laughed and told him that was normal. They'd always thought the people in the walls were just regular people, except that they were smaller and they made "sacrifices".

Which we learned about at school when we were talking about the Mayans.

Who made sacrifices all the time.

Which didn't make them bad, just different.

Which my mom and grandma explained to Dad.

My grandpa said the people in the walls didn't have jobs, and called them "communists," but I don't know what that means.

My mom says none of this made my dad feel better.

My mom says he spent the rest of the day staring at the walls, jumping when anyone said his name.

My mom says she caught him scratching at a rip in the wallpaper once.

My mom says he didn't want to go to bed.

My mom says they lay there together in the dark, talking, and she promised she'd stay up with him.

My mom says she feels bad about it, but she drifted off again, leaving him alone, staring at the ceiling.

My dad says he thought about shaking her awake, but something told him not to.

My dad says he didn't move a muscle all night.

My dad says he heard them again, and he could hear them so clearly that he could picture what was happening in his head, step by step, when they did the butchering.

They'd chant, "This is our choice. This is our choice. This is our choice."

They'd tear and break and crush and twist and rip.

They'd press the sacrifice's eyes back into the sockets until the eyes popped, then they'd tape the mouth shut (he says he could hear the peel of the duct tape).

They'd saw open the neck and then tape that shut, too, so the sacrifice bled into their throat and drowned in it, and because their hands were already twisted off, they couldn't take off the tape so they'd just wriggle around like worms until they died.

Then the people in the walls all said good night, very formally, and went to bed.

My mom says he didn't need to tell me that part.

My dad says it's the only part that matters.

Which always makes my mom angry.

Which makes my dad stop talking.

My dad says, at the time, he didn't know why they killed their own, how they chose the sacrifice, or what they did with the bodies.

Which he says he imagined simply piling up behind the walls, for years and years, slowly filling the house until the walls warped and small person parts began sliding out through cracks in the wallpaper.

Which he told my mom.

Which she was nervous about, because she was scared that she was scaring him away.

Which she tried not to do, by assuring him that the people in the walls just had a very different way of life.

Part of which must have been eating their own.

Which must have been where the bodies went.

Which she assured him is perfectly natural—lots of cultures eat strange things, including dogs and people.

Which my dad says he asked my grandpa about.

Which my grandpa denied, because the small people sounded much too polite to eat their own, despite all that killing they did very regularly.

Which my grandpa almost said more about, but stopped himself.

Which made my dad *really* wonder where the bodies went.

Dad says he spent several days sitting in a chair in the corner while Mom ran around the house, trying to find the Santa figurines.

Dad says she asked him to join her, but he couldn't.

Dad says he was too scared to even think.

A few days into the trip, he went looking for Grandma Ellen, who he found in the attic.

Which is where he found her kneeling by a small metal latch in the wall.

Which was about three inches tall, and which was in the wall right by the floor.

Which he says she had open, and was scooping something out of.

Which, when he got closer, he saw was parts.

Arms. Legs. Heads.

Small person parts.

Which made him want to throw up.

Which made my grandma get a chair and tell him to sit down.

Which he did, as he waited for her to get him a glass of water.

He stared at the small open door, and at the little basket of parts she'd been scooping (all the fingers and feet sticking out), until she came back.

Which she did, carrying a glass of water he was too scared to drink.

Which is when she explained about the limbs.

Which started, she said, when my mom was in middle school.

Grandma said, one day after my mom came home from school, she and my mom were wondering about the people in the walls and wanted to know what they looked like.

"They seem so sweet," my grandma said. "Saying good night so politely every night, and making tea."

My mom, who hated the sound of the kettle when they made tea because it woke her up (which I said already), only half agreed.

"But," she said, "I *do* think I'd like to meet them one day. Maybe peel apart the walls and look inside."

Which gave them both the same idea at the same time.

Which led to them tearing apart a wall in the kitchen that very minute, giggling and looking around with flashlights.

Which revealed hundreds upon hundreds of people, each about a foot tall, hanging from beams like bats, arms crossed over their chests, fast asleep. They were dressed very nicely, in vests and trousers and house dresses and pant suits and gowns and tuxedos and all kinds of things. Even a monocle or two.

Which my mom thought was just adorable.

Which is why she took one.

Then they covered up the wall hole with cardboard, nailing it in place.

The person she took screamed and squealed and kicked, even bit. My mom tried to keep it in a glass jar but it suffocated (which my dad says means "ran out of air"), so she had to get another one.

Which she did by peeling up the nails in the cardboard, plucking another person out of the wall, and putting the cardboard back in place, holding in one hand the still-sleeping person.

Which, according to my grandma, she kept in a terrarium.

Which lasted a while, until the small person broke their head against the glass wall and killed themselves.

Which led to my mom taking another. And then another. And another. All of them killed themselves, or died by accident. One made a rope from her little pants and hung herself in the cage.

"Some people keep guinea pigs, or fish," my grandma explained to my dad. "They die all the time. It's not any different. Pets are hard."

But my grandma started feeling really bad that my mom couldn't keep any of them alive.

So she took the most recently dead one, fixed it up, and dipped it in glaze, then baked it, turning the person into a little ceramic figurine. Keeping it locked in the same little position forever.

My grandma surprised her with the first one, and then dipped the next dead pet (which came a few days later) in the glaze, too, so the first would have a friend on the shelf. They posed them together on the mantel, my dad told me. Two little figures waving at each other. Then my grandma and mom started taking people out of the walls and making figurines together, which became their favorite thing to do together.

But the small people got tired of this. They got tired of losing people at random all the time. So every morning, they chose one of their own and served them up in the attic.

"Isn't that a hoot?" my grandma said to my dad, laughing.

He wanted to know why they killed each other so violently.

Grandma Ellen said the butchering was actually very helpful because it made turning the people into figurines much easier. This way, my mom and grandma didn't have to scoop out the blood or the eyes or try moving the limbs through "rigor mortis" (which is when a dead body gets too stiff to move). They just had a bunch of parts they could adjust like they wanted. The people in the walls did it to "appease" Mom and Grandma Ellen, which means make them happy.

"They think we're gods," Grandma Ellen told my dad.

Which I understand, because of the Mayans.

I asked my dad why he was never really into the figurines, and he gave me a strange look.

I asked him why he decided to stay with Mom if he didn't like them so much.

Which is when he told me that my mom told him that if he tried to leave, she'd sacrifice him to the giants.

"You're *my* choice," she told him.

He said that made him nervous.

I asked him if she meant she'd sacrifice him just like the small people did.

Which is when his eyes got really wide and he said, "Yes, but Ellie—*everybody* is the small people."

"But we're not small," I told him.

"Yes, we are," he said.

"But we don't live in walls," I told him. "There aren't any giant people around."

"We *do* live in walls," he said.

He told me that every so often, the giants pick someone. They bring them up out of the wall, they fix them up, and dip them in ceramic. They pose them however they want. Sometimes, if the giants are taking too many people, it's easier to sacrifice someone. If someone's really old or really sick, we sacrifice them to the giants.

My dad says that's what happened to my grandpa.

My dad says he had Alzheimer's, which is when your brain rots before your body does.

My dad says he asked to go.

My dad says they all got together in the living room and cut him up. Dad couldn't do it, so he was the one who handled the duct tape.

Which he also almost couldn't do.

My mom popped the eyes, he says, and Grandma Ellen twisted off the hands.

Which he says is the worst thing he ever saw.

Which he says was only made worse by my mom and my grandma chanting as they worked.

"This is our choice. This is our choice. This is our choice."

He says he felt watched by the people in the walls. He says he felt their fingers wriggling at the boards, pushing their faces against the wallpaper and trying to see. He could feel hundreds of curious faces looking at him from all around the room.

He says once they'd butchered my grandpa, they got all the pieces in a basket and then hauled the basket outside.

He says they carried it into the woods.

He says they got the basket on a rope and pulley on one of the trees.

He says they worked the rope and hiked the basket up the tree.

He says that after ten minutes of work, the basket disappeared into the mist.

He says that they could feel something tugging on the rope, up there, beyond where they could see, at the very top of the world.

He says that when they pulled the basket back down, it was empty.

Which is why, he told me, he went nuts and burned my grandma's house to the ground.

Which he says was terrible, because he had to make sure he didn't get caught, and because he could hear all the little voices in the walls screaming.

He says he could see their little hands flailing outside the wallpaper.

He says he could hear their bodies burning.

He says he could see them tumbling out of the walls as they died.

Melting, bleeding, and popping like cooked sausages.

He says he felt bad that Grandma got trapped in the fire, too.

He says he doesn't feel *that* bad, though.

All of which he says I am never allowed to tell my mom.

Ever.

Ever.

Ever.

Which I told him I wouldn't.

Which is also why he doesn't like to go in my room.

He doesn't like to think about the figurines in my room.

He doesn't like to think about where my mom keeps getting them.

He doesn't like to think about how I get one every year for my birthday, and how sometimes my mom will surprise me with one at random.

But my mom just says that's because he's not open to new experiences.

Because he's "grounded."

My mom says that when I hear our house settling at night, it's not the house at all.

She says it's the people in the walls.

My dad says that's not true. He says it's the house moving of its own accord, and his hands shake when he says this.

My mom says that's ridiculous because no house does anything of its own accord, and there are no accidents, there are only things that the people in our walls do not want us to see.

My mom says that *every* house acts according to the people in its walls.

That even *our* house acts according to the people in its walls.

That Dad should be careful, or she'll sacrifice him to the giants, and feed his parts to them in a basket, which they'll haul all the way up a tree so someone larger than us can scoop them out of a latch in the attic.

Just like Grandpa.

Which my dad never says anything to.

Which makes my mom laugh, and then she ruffles his hair and says she loves him.

Which she also says to me. "I love you."

Especially when she gives me a new figurine.

Which is all the time.

Sometimes, I stay up and try to hear the small people in *our* walls.

Sometimes I listen very hard.

But I never hear anything.

My dad says this is because they're scared, and don't want to be found.

My dad says they're scared of people like Mom, and Grandma, and me.

My dad says I shouldn't like the figurines.

My dad says it's cruel.

But I think Mom's right.

I think he's not thinking about it the right way.

Plus, Mom says I'm almost the same age she was when she started.

Mom says, soon, she'll show me the hole in the attic where she gets the parts.

Mom says she'll show me how to use a knife, so I can help take care of Dad when he gets old and sick.

Mom says she's excited to show me how to make my own figurines.

Mom says it's like having a Mr. Potato-Head, and you always have new ones to play with.

Which I'm excited for, too.

I like Mr. Potato-Head.

And I like ceramic figurines.

■

Sam Rebelein recently graduated from Goddard College with an MFA in Creative Writing. His work has previously appeared in Shimmer, Dark Moon Digest, Every Day Fiction, *and elsewhere. He lives in Brooklyn and on Twitter @HillaryScruff.*

GIVING A BLOOD TRANSFUSION TO A STONE

—■—

Jonathan Plombon

1. TALKING OUT OF YOUR SHELL

A turtle named Indolent sat hunched over in the corner of the room, with his chair pressed so far back against the wall that it routinely chipped off the white paint, allowing the plaster to glide to the carpeted ground like a torn pillow weeping feathered tears. He was human-sized. Not that a human-sized turtle was an uncommon sight in the therapy group, as the group also attracted two clams, three hermit crabs and six armadillos who all hovered above six feet. Being around others that shared the same affliction was of little relief to Indolent, who avoided making eye contact with anyone else for fear that they would attempt to talk to him. He wasn't alone. The group was for "those wanting to break out of their shells."

2. SHE FANTASIZED ABOUT HER MOTHER'S PICTURE BEING ON A MILK CARTON

The mental health center, and the therapy groups held within it, did not just accommodate those wishing to break out of their shells. It also assisted those who had a nagging feeling that something was always missing. That therapy group focused mostly on those who suffered from abandonment issues, although one human woman, who admitted that there was something missing, had no idea exactly what she was missing. The head of the group, a life-sized self-help book called "Why There's a Light Switch in Your Stomach: Finding the Power in You," suggested that it could be connected to her strained relationship with her mother.

That human woman's name was Magnificent.

"My relationship with my mother is not missing," she told the group. "I know where it is. Believe me, I'm not missing my relationship with my mother. Not at all."

"Then you may have to look harder than the others to find what you don't have," the book said. "We're all dealing with the same issues. I'll make a confession."

The book took a deep breath.

"I'm abridged. There are things that I just don't make public," the book said. "I'm also dating someone who's illiterate, which makes it very difficult for him to read me."

Magnificent thought about it, running her hand around her face, stopping to rub the early morning out of her eyes before moving her fingers to itch her nose and pinch her own cheeks. When she yawned, Magnificent thought that it was too early for this kind of crap. That was true, but it could have been 7 p.m. and it would still be too early for any of this crap.

Her soda can sat on the floor directly beneath her. She hunched over like a turtle in a therapy group and lifted it to her mouth. Four droplets of Pepsi fell out of the top of the can and ended up on the panties that covered her chest.

It was always such a pain to drink, and eat for that matter, with no lips.

3. LIKE GENITALIA, FEELINGS SHOULD NOT BE EXPOSED IN PUBLIC

Feelings aren't social creatures. They're bottled up. They're kept inside. While this lifestyle entails a great deal of loneliness, feelings actually utilize loneliness as a survival mechanism. Without which, feelings are at much higher risk of getting hurt.

This is not a physical type of harm, because there are laws to discourage physical harm. There are laws against kicking Benji and Johnny Depp. There are no such laws against hurting Benji and Johnny Depp's feelings.

Furthermore, there are no hospitals for feelings. When a feeling is hurt, it cannot go to a doctor. And feelings are not protected. Police won't arrest anyone for hurting a feeling.

Feelings don't go out very often. It's safer that way.

4. A Chance at an Opportunity

As the group disbanded for the day, Indolent mapped out his future plans. He felt encouraged by the progress he was making, not in the group, of which there was little, but with the speed he was physically moving. By Indolent's calculation, he could walk (upright, as he learned how to do in order to be tall enough to make it on carnival rides) home in two days, which felt very short, since it was the fastest he could move. It also felt very long, since it would take two days to reach his home, and, much like all turtles, his home was the shell on his back.

By the door of the mental health center, Indolent noticed Magnificent hurling her arms in the air, looking as if she were practicing the motion of throwing. However, she had nothing in her hands. She spun around, whirling like a top, without regard to the space around her, and fell into Indolent. He collapsed on his back and wiggled, unable to pick himself up by his own power.

"I'm sorry," Magnificent exclaimed, pulling him back up. "I should be more careful about this stuff."

Indolent realized that meeting Magnificent might be an opportunity. He heard about these. He almost never came across opportunities. And he almost never took chances. He saw neither chances nor opportunities enough to know when he saw one, especially when it came to the opposite sex. Attention from the opposite sex was just as hard to come by.

He also couldn't tell if this was the kind of attention that came from someone who voluntarily gave it, or the type of attention that was given because it was mandatory, like a woman who works at McDonald's and has to smile at every customer.

"It's okay," Indolent sputtered. "What were you doing?"

"I'm practicing throwing my mother under the bus," Magnificent said. "You have to practice to keep yourself in shape for when the time comes. Opportunities rarely present themselves. I don't get many."

She didn't get many opportunities, either. They have something in common, Indolent thought. He beamed.

"I'm getting better. My hope is that if I stand close enough to the wheels of the bus, that the bus will just back up to compensate for my lack of throwing distance," she said then hesitated. "You don't have lips."

"You either," he said.

"That's more than 95% of all couples have in common," Magnificent said. "What happened to yours?"

"I was born this way," he responded, then realized that the woman just used the word *couple*. "What about you?"

"My mother is a psychic, which is awful. I used to get grounded for something I'd do two weeks later," Magnificent said.

Indolent just nodded his head. He didn't know how to respond to what she'd just said.

"Anyway, my mother didn't read palms. She read lips. She read my lips, which I can't remember exactly what my lips said, but I'm sure she didn't think it was flattering. I don't agree with her about what I said. I doubt it was as bad as she thinks, but I guess she would know better than I do, because she is, after all, psychic and would know that I did something wrong before I would do anything wrong," Magnificent said. "So, I made my lips disappear. That way she couldn't read them. Most magicians make an entire person or the Statue of Liberty disappear. I made my lips disappear and I feel lucky that I even got that to work."

Indolent nodded.

"So, do you throw your mother under a bus, too?" Magnificent asked.

"No," he answered. "I don't know where my mother is."

"Is she in the bathroom?"

"Oh, I mean that I don't know where she is in the world. I never knew her."

"Oh, I'm sorry," Magnificent said. "How about your father?"

"No," he said. "I can never find him when a bus is nearby."

5. WHAT TO EXPECT WHEN YOU'RE EXPECTING YOUR SON TO BE A TOTAL FAILURE

Indolent's father once gave him *the talk* when Indolent was 36.

The type of conversation that is conducted when the child is 36 differs slightly from the one when the child is 10. When the child is 10, the talk features the child asking the parent questions. These questions are along the lines of "What's menstruation?" When the child is 36, the parent asks the child questions. These questions are along the lines of "Are you ever going to start bringing women home?"

This can be followed up by a number of questions, or rather statements, by the parent, including "There are late bloomers and then there are never bloomers" and "I don't want my son to be a never bloomer" and "Greg's son was a late bloomer. Now look at him. He's bloomed."

"Greg's son is a red spider lily. They can only bloom in fall. Besides, it's nature. He has to bloom eventually," Indolent said to his father. "I don't."

6. WHEN TOLD TO MAKE SOMETHING OF HERSELF, MAGNIFICENT MADE HERSELF A MESS

After an exchange of names, and the proper introduction completed, Indolent gathered all of his courage to extend the conversation. He didn't know what subjects were appropriate, which led to him second guessing everything he was about to say, which resulted in long periods of silence.

He had questions, mainly about her appearance. Although Magnificent was human (her hands, feet, stomach, and facial features gave that away), she otherwise was constructed of various items. Her arms were failed report cards, as well as mug shots from the times she was arrested for public intoxication. In the place usually reserved for her chest, Magnificent had stained underwear from when she accidently urinated during math class in the third grade. Another pair, from when she wet herself at Melissa Hockenpower's sleepover, could also be seen. A dead fetus, from an abortion when she was 26, made up half of her right thigh. Other items, many difficult to identify, and many she didn't want to attempt to identify, filled her out

"What's the worst thing about not having lips for you?" Indolent asked.

"I guess it's not being able to smile," she responded. "I wish I could smile. I'd like to smile at someone, especially to the people who work at those fast-food joints. They could use a smile. Actually, I wish I would have given them mine. Not all of them at once. I doubt that everyone could have used my smile at the same time. It wasn't *that* big. Maybe they could all share it. Or trade it off every week or maybe every shift. Give it to whoever was working the register."

Indolent nodded. He didn't know how the respond.

"Then again, I also can't frown. That's a plus," she said. "But then again, again, it's not like I don't get depressed. I just can't show it."

As often was the case, Indolent told himself to make some sort audible reaction, rather than just shrugging or nodding his head. And as was often the case with the previous case, he ended up just shrugging and nodding his head.

"I'm a magician," Magnificent blurted out, thankfully eliminating Indolent's need to make any additional topics of conversation. "At least, I'm a magician who has never really had any magic. Not with any assistants that I've ever had. Compatibility between an assistant and a magician is of the utmost importance. People think that magic and science are mutually exclusive, but they're actually connected. You can't have any magic with a person if you don't first have chemistry."

"Does biology play a factor when looking for an assistant?" Indolent asked.

"Only to the superficial," Magnificent responded.

7. WHEN YOUR LINKEDIN PROFILE DOUBLES AS YOUR MATCH.COM PROFILE

Prior to meeting Indolent, Magnificent tried out a number of assistants with no real success. Magnificent's mother told her that she needed to reconsider her definition of *magic*. "You have to be realistic," Magnificent's mother said. "Maybe you won't be able to whisk an assistant off his feet. Maybe the world won't move each time that you touch him. You tried so hard to make that one assistant work out. You wanted to make his heart pound right out of his chest. Forget out of his chest, you couldn't even make his heart pound."

"He was dead," Magnificent replied.

"Before or after you were done with him?" her mother responded.

8. It Should be Noted That Indolent Is Not a Licensed Real Estate Agent

Indolent designed his home, otherwise known as the shell on his back, with logic and practicality. He didn't add anything that wouldn't be used or anything that didn't serve a purpose to a feeling.

Feelings enjoy the privacy of a bomb shelter. When a bomb shelter is no longer a viable option, due to the demand outweighing the quantity, feelings seek out alternative forms of housing.

Indolent had a feeling. One. He had one feeling. And that feeling had begun renting an alternative to a bomb shelter: Indolent's shell home.

When Indolent showed his home to his feeling, he made it a point to emphasize the hiding spots. As Indolent said to his feeling, "The property has many hiding spots that might be to your liking such as the space underneath the bed and the six locked closets. By the way, each closet can hold up to twelve skeletons. Those are luxury closets."

With that in mind, Indolent didn't furnish the home with a bedroom, a bathroom or a kitchen. Indolent, instead, added a space under the bed (but not the bed itself since it served no function), several dark corners and a few closets for the feelings to hide in and on. There was also a dressing room, which was a necessity since feelings change so often.

Not that the feeling could just walk out. The only way that a feeling can leave its home is if it's shared. It could be shared at any moment that there's another being around. There had been thousands of beings in close proximity to Indolent over the past 36 years. He never shared any of his feelings with any of them. His feelings stayed indoors.

Selfish as he may appear to be, he didn't want to share his feelings with anyone. That was always the case. When the other children in kindergarten brought in toys and games for show and tell, Indolent brought his feelings. But when the teacher advised him to share his feelings with the other children, Indolent held them inside and wouldn't let anyone near them.

9. A REVELATION THE LIKES OF WHICH WE HAVE NOT SEEN SINCE THE BIBLE

"What do you miss most about not having lips?" Magnificent asked.

"I can't miss what I never had," Indolent responded.

"What do you think you would miss if you had lips?"

"Probably kissing."

"It is pretty difficult to kiss someone without lips," she said. "At least, you can get kissed."

"That's never happened," Indolent said.

"You've never been kissed?" Magnificent asked.

10. The Birds, The Bees and The Rabbits

Indolent's father knew about the birds and the bees.

He was a rabbit.

Indolent's father had 300 children. Two-hundred-ninety-nine of them were rabbits. One of those children was a turtle. Indolent was that turtle.

"Why can't you be like your 299 brothers?" Indolent's father asked him. "They've all been in relationships. I'm a grandfather 700 times over."

11. The Special Skills That Employers Look For

In some countries, feelings aren't allowed to participate in the schoolyard game called hide and seek. This is due to them having an unfair advantage in the game. Feelings hiding themselves is a distinctive trait of their species, akin to how kangaroos are famous for hopping or fish are known for swimming.

Kangaroos hop. Fish swim. Feelings hide.

It's just safer that way.

12. If You Love Something, Set It Free

"I mostly make things disappear. My paycheck for one," Magnificent said.

"If you can make things disappear, wouldn't you be able to make them reappear?" Indolent asked.

"If I know where they ended up, then, sure, maybe. Like I know where my paycheck goes when that disappears," she said.

"Where's that?"

"Taco Bell, but they never give me my money back, since I've already eaten all of it," Magnificent said. "If you'd like, I can show you how to make something disappear."

Magnificent took her soda can and placed it behind her back. With a ta-da, she pulled the soda can back out.

"It didn't work," he said.

"Yes, it did," she answered.

"The can is still there."

"It wasn't the can that disappeared," she said. "It was my confidence. Every time I fuck up a trick, I lose even more."

Indolent nodded his head. He didn't know that losing confidence was a trick. He had been losing confidence in himself for years. It didn't seem so magical to him.

"Do you want me to make the soda can disappear?" Magnificent asked.

Indolent nodded.

"It's all about magic words," she said. "You can make anything happen with the right words."

So, she said, "I love you," to the can.

The can dematerialized, vanished into the air like a ghost that realizes it's not real.

"Everything disappears when you love it," Magnificent said.

13. AND IF YOU HATE SOMETHING, YOU SHOULD ALSO LET IT GO

When Magnificent learned that reciting those words would cause something to vanish, she finally told her mother that she loved her. Often. Repeatedly. Over and over again. You have to at least act like you mean the words, however, and she was just a magician. Not an actress.

14. WITH A SLEIGHT OF HAND AND DECADES OF THERAPY

"If you made your lips disappear, can you make them reappear?" Indolent asked.

"Maybe," she said. "I can never seem to get rid of anything that I don't want. That's why I look like this. That's why I have my dead child on my thigh. That's why I'm made out of cars. Not just any cars. The ones that I drove into the sides of garages. And I'm also made out of videos, the surveillance ones that feature me yelling at a customer when I worked at Arby's."

"I don't follow," Indolent said, as he had said, and thought, many times before.

Magnificent held her palm over her mouth then lowered it to reveal her mother in the space usually reserved for her lips. She never wanted her mother to be her lips. So, of course, her mother became her lips. Go figure.

Before, Magnificent's mother didn't like what her daughter's lips would say. Now, Magnificent's mother was her lips. And they wouldn't say, or do, anything that conflicted with her mother's standards.

"I have to be your mother, your advisor, your alibi, your loan officer," her mother said. "And now I have to be your lips. You can't depend on me for everything. I won't be around forever, you know. Just because I'm your mother, it doesn't mean that ..."

15. When a Turtle Tells You That You Need to Take Things Slower

This was all happening too quickly, especially for a turtle. He just met this woman and now he was already meeting her mother.

16. When Your Mother Says, "One Day I'll be Gone," and You Respond with "Can That One Day be Today?"

"... I should do everything for you. You have to grow up sometime. I'm only being hard on you because you'll have to fend for yourself in life. One day I will not be here. You did this to yourself. You chose to get rid of your lips. This was your doing. I didn't tell you to get rid of your lips. I'm ..." Magnificent's mother continued.

17. Abandonment Issues.
Abandonment Subscriptions.

It was the first night in her new home for Indolent's feeling. She didn't own it; she only rented it, but it made her feel protected. The only door in the house was locked. The windows served no other purpose than to allow its occupant to see just how intimidating the outside world could be.

The price of rent was her freedom. Other than that, she considered the rent pretty reasonable.

Feelings hide out of fear that they could get lost. Search parties provide little help. They can never find the right feeling. Feelings are so easy to lose; they're camouflage. They leave. They are not loyal.

You can lose a feeling. And when that happens, you might never have that feeling again.

18. It's Still Pretty Impressive for an Upright Turtle to Dance at All

"Sometimes I feel like I don't pick up on stuff. Not right away, anyway. I'm slow. I never know what to do," Indolent said.

"I can help you with that," she said. "Sometimes people need to be led. It's their purpose in the world. You can't have someone leading unless you have someone who needs to be led."

Neither said a word, although millions of words ran through their heads. Most of the words told them to say something.

"I can lead," Magnificent said, as she placed her hand on his shell. "Dance with me."

She began to move, in a tangle of sweaty palms and sweaty feet and the general awkwardness of finger placement between a turtle and a human who want nothing more than to make it perfect and find that accidentally squeezing too tight around the shell of a giant turtle, and the impending nervous giggling from the slightly painful mishap, was actually as perfect as it could ever be.

"I'm starting to slip," he said.

"I got you," she said. "I'll support you. Just lean on me."

"I think I'm falling," he said, attempting to get his footing.

"Me too," she said, holding him up.

19. ACCURATE

Feelings look like a cross between an open wound and a closed door.

20. WHEN SOMEONE STEPS ON YOUR TOES AND YOU'RE JUST HAPPY THAT YOU HAVE TOES FOR SOMEONE TO STEP ON

"I don't know how to dance," Indolent said.

"Neither do I," she said, then laughed, falling forward and tapping her head against his chest. And with that they moved their feet. Not anywhere in particular nor with any music, at least at first, but as they continued to move everywhere and anywhere, cracking more than a few of Magnificent's toenails, they got in a rhythm with each step providing a drum beat, every *ouch* they uttered turning into an off-key vocal track, and all the wind flowing through their tunnel vision becoming a remarkable imitation of a violin.

21. "I'll Take You Right into the Comfort Zone" by Kenny Loggins

Even feelings have feelings. And Indolent's feeling had a feeling she wanted to finally leave.

Indolent wouldn't allow it.

Indolent had a history of being rather selfish. He kept all of his feelings to himself. He never shared them with any of the other children. His first-grade teacher often expressed her frustration about it to Indolent's father, who did nothing about it. His father was often too busy to read the notes sent home from school, since he had 299 other children to neglect.

But the feeling wanted to be shared — with or without Indolent's permission.

It crawled from out of the corner.

22. You Don't Perform Magic; You Feel It

When Indolent and Magnificent stopped dancing, which was a result of Indolent nearly colliding with a passing therapist, he blushed to such an extent that it raised his internal temperature so high that it made parts of his face melt.

"Ta-daaaa," Magnificent said, surprised by her own ability to heat things up.

"I'm falling again," he said.

"I was kind of hoping you never stopped."

They both leaned in. Magnificent knew that she would be responsible for most of the work, seeing as she had the lips to kiss, and she puckered up as she approached his face. Indolent attempted to just stand still, although his heart's pounding was so loud it made him jump. It was as if he had never experienced it before. Maybe he hadn't. A working heart meant that he was alive, which he had doubts about for years.

She inched nearer, as did Indolent in an effort to expedite the process. He didn't want to miss this opportunity. He could never capitalize on opportunities or chances. He moved too slow. He thought too slow. He wasn't a rabbit. Rabbits were fast. And despite what the fable said, a turtle could never catch up to a rabbit. But that wouldn't stop him. Not this time.

23. A Minimum-Security Death Row with a Stringent Honor System

Indolent's feeling gripped the doorknob, turning it. It squeaked like a mouse noticing too late that the cheese lay on a trap.

The feeling opened up the front door. It turned out the door wasn't locked. It had been open the entire time. The feeling just had to try.

24. A Scream in a World Without Ears

Indolent left his eyes open. He felt that if he closed them, he'd open them back up and she'd be gone.

Nonetheless, there was a disappearance. Even with his eyes opened.

Magnificent didn't vanish, but her lips did. She had wanted them to stay, but her mother wouldn't be a willing participant in the mistake that her daughter was committing.

"I didn't say, 'I love you,'" Indolent said.

"You didn't have to," Magnificent responded. "I already knew it."

They pulled away from each other.

"But just your lips disappeared, not your entire body. I don't love just your lips. I love you. Shouldn't you completely disappear?"

"Just wait," Magnificent said. "I'll leave. It'll happen soon enough."

25. It's Just Safer That Way

Indolent's feeling turned back into the house and crawled into the closet. She locked the door behind her.

26. INDOLENT ASKS A QUESTION WITH NO RIGHT ANSWER

"What happened?" Indolent asked.

27. HER MOTHER'S CONSULTATION FIRM WAS LOCATED IN THE HEART OF THE PEANUT GALLERY

"I told you that you would drive him away," her mother said. "Just like all of them."

28. MAGNIFICENT CORRECTLY ANSWERS INDOLENT'S QUESTION WITH ONLY WRONG ANSWERS

"The magic," Magnificent said to Indolent, "is gone."

29. "I'M MOVING AS SLOW AS I CAN GO," HER PATIENCE SAID

Magnificent turned and walked away.

Indolent thought about going after her, but he knew, with Magnificent having a two-step head start, that he would never catch up to her.

He was just too slow. At everything. He didn't kiss her quickly enough. In fact, he didn't kiss her at all. He couldn't. And he waited too long to make a move. And he didn't think of the right thing to say.

He was just too slow.

30. "I'M NOT LOCATED IN THE PEANUT GALLERY LIKE PEOPLE THINK," HER MOM SAID. "YOU CAN FIND ME IN YOUR EAR."

"... just saying that you should think for yourself. Find your way. Find your own personality. Reach your own conclusions. You should stop listening to everyone and forge your own way in life," Magnificent's mother said.

31. MOVING ON IS DIFFICULT FOR ANYONE ENDING A RELATIONSHIP

Magnificent had feelings of her own. She always kept hers in the pit of her stomach, which is where Magnificent retreated back to after she walked away from Indolent. Upon arriving in the pit of her own stomach, she noticed her mother holding a syringe of Novocain up to her feelings.

"Is this yours?" her mother asked.

"Yeah, I mean kind of," she stumbled and stuttered. "They're feelings. I mean they were going to be gifts. They were feelings for someone else."

Magnificent jumped in front of the syringe, causing her mother to lower her arms. The daughter motioned with her hand to give up the piercing instrument, which her mother did after a few seconds of trading looks between her daughter and her daughter's feelings. When Magnificent got control of the shot, she pointed it at her feelings, the ones for Indolent, and thrust, shoving the Novocain into her feelings, making her feelings feel no more

"It saves so much time if I just do it myself," Magnificent said.

32. "It Looks Great. It's So You."

Another item appeared on her body: a picture of Indolent waiting for his kiss.

■

Jonathan Plombon is a writer from Minnesota. His work has appeared in Bombay Gin, Quarter After Eight, The Journal of Experimental Fiction, *and other publications. He enjoys watching professional wrestling and waking up in the middle of the night to find that he has three more hours to sleep.*

THE ARBORISTS

■

Rebecca Bennett

Never plan for the smoothest cut.

Even before the whistle of the bone flute reaches its highest pitch, Craig has the gold paint smeared across his nose. He's off and running, vanished. Already deep in the forest, darting between the trees. Like always, there is no hesitation to my brother's movements. He's swift and sure. Confident in a way that I can only guess. The sound of the whistle is carved into his bones, childhood memories writ into muscle. When Craig was younger, he'd wear the full costume, hiding under the skin of a deer with his face fully painted gold, but now just a faint swipe of gold is all he allows.

Another whistle, this time further away. The sound is sharper. It doesn't echo through the trees. Instead the sound hangs in the air, heavy and thick as fog. The forest stills, waiting. My father and I don't move. Even breathing seems too disruptive. My legs tense, aching with the desire to follow the sound as well. To race into the forest and lose myself. The oak tree begins to rustle, its leaves shake, rattling in tune with the vibration of the pitch.

The bark of the tree splits and opens, glowing as the wisp of a dryad is drawn out. It follows Craig as he runs through the woods.

If you don't draw out the dryad before you cut the oak, the sap turns red and stains the wood. Unstained oak is worth a fortune. There are acres of trees in the bush, but tricking a spirit is always a dangerous prospect. Untrained woodcutters die every year, so many waltz out into the forest with a painted flute looking for their fortune. Worse than the missing bodies are the half-chopped trees left to decay. Stained wood is useless, never fully drying. The sap hardens like crystal until the wood splits.

There's the barest glow of the dryad through the trees as she chases my brother. The chain saw pitches as it makes the backcut, piercing through the middle and then out the side of the tree. The ax is by my father's feet, ready to be grabbed the moment the tree falls so we can free it completely. He's more than halfway through when I hear the three warning whistles of my brother.

Something has gone wrong.

The chain saw stops.

Every spring I worry a little more. Craig is fast, but middle-age is something you can't outrun. If he's caught, there's no goodbye, no body. My brother will vanish and become another system of roots added to the forest floor.

"Beth." Dad shouts until I turn to face him. His face is red from exertion and cold. The chain saw is still halfway through the tree. He's so close to being done, stopping now would waste the wood. We'd be destroying a home for no reason at all.

"There's not much more to go. Get to Craig, I'll finish off the tree. Everything will be fine. Okay, Bethie? Get Craig. Everything will be fine."

At his nod, I race into the trees. The chain saw echoes behind me, loud and violent. Even as I run further from the site, I can still hear the shatter of the bark. The chips of wood scattering into the air. From the moment the cutting begins, the dryad will either continue her hunt or return home to protect her tree.

From here on out it's just timing. Either my father will finish or the dryad will. There's no in-between: The tree is upright or it's on the ground. Beyond the whine of the chain saw, there's a higher pitched noise. One that only I can hear.

The forest hums around me. Pushing me to run faster, run deeper. I spot my brother's yellow fleece but my legs have trouble slowing. A switch clicks on in the back of my mind, something primitive and selfish. It wants speed and wind. It almost hurts to slow and veer course. Stumbling, nearly tripping across exposed roots, I slow enough to fall to my knees next to Craig. The cold, wetness of mud and dead leaves soak through my jeans.

"Craig?" I didn't expect to find him—not really. When things go wrong out in the bush, they really go wrong. We're hours away from any town. Craig is shaking, his arm bent at a strange angle. He's injured, but he should be dead. "What happened? Are you okay?"

"I fell." Craig's face is bloodless. The paleness makes him look older. He could be a stranger, all sweaty and wheezing.

It feels wrong. A dryad never abandons her hunt, not when she's that close. We've lost our own in these woods before. Our blood is sewn into the soil. Granddad hadn't been too far from the work site either when a dryad caught him. Grandma said she knew the moment it happened, it didn't matter that she had been washing dishes miles away. It took months before I could speak to her again. I had hated her soft, weighty form that was built for hugs but not for running. She wanted walls and children, but she should have been in the forest. She'd have heard the song; perhaps she could have changed it.

Craig loops his good arm around me and we struggle to stand. Once he's up, his back is stiff. He's not leaning into me as much as he should. "Is it here? Can you see it?"

There's no glowing wisp. But the humming in the base of my spine tells me that the dryad is still alive. She's circling maybe. Either us or the tree. We need to move faster.

"Did dad finish cutting? I tried to give you as much time before—"

"No, he's still working on it." We hobble together, moving as fast as we can. There's still chainsawing in the distance. It doesn't make sense – the dryads have never waited this long to defend their home before. The closer we get to the site, the more the humming strengthens until I can feel the thrum in my chest. She's here, somewhere. Just watching us.

The site is visible through the trees. The oak has slanted to the left, my father still working at the base. By the time we make it to the edge of camp, the tree is already in motion. The hinge of wood and bark bends. Cracking and splintering up the length until it folds in on itself. It falls with a sharp crack. There's a finality to the thud when it hits the ground.

My spine tingles. I don't need to turn around to know the dryad returned. She's too late, I know that by the chop of the ax. But dryads always return to their tree when it dies. Neither my father nor brother can hear the hum. They don't see the waning figure of the dryad. The burst of green that shapes itself into a woman's form, she'll shrink and harden until an acorn falls to the ground in her place. To them she's already gone, lost in the debris that carpets the forest's floor. There's still a faint hum, muted like it's been buried. I know she'll return one day, growing stronger until the next generation cuts her again.

Craig pulls away, almost falling into our father's open arms. Dad claps him on the back, careful to avoid the injured arm. When dad lets go, Craig steps back, avoiding both of our gazes and rubs the gold paint from his face.

"I'll cut up the trunk and then we'll go," Dad says quietly. "It's was close today, too close. What happened?"

Craig shrugs, his ears are flushed. He's still looking out into the trees instead of at us. "I fell." There's something he's not saying. Probably some embarrassment like a bum knee or other marker of age that he wants to ignore. We're all older than we'd like to admit. Forty is closing in; I never had the patience to hide the gray or cover my lines.

There's a scratch from a rock or branch on the top of my brother's head, visible now that he's losing hair. He's been planning for his sons to be down here next summer as spotters. If they do well enough they might become runners soon too. Craig has never said that he'd prefer I stayed home, like my grandmother did before me. The hesitation, when he calls me out to the carriage, the too-quick snap of a closed door, speaks clearly enough.

Dad frowns but doesn't ask again. "Okay, I can ask Uncle Steve, or someone else, to help out next time." Uncle Steve is younger than dad, he's in better shape but still pushing 50. It already feels too dangerous.

Craig shakes his head. "No. It's a good day; it'll be week before we get another day like this."

The season for cutting oaks is almost over, the harsh winter kept us out of the woods far too long. We can't just pick and choose whatever trees to cut. There's a system, you switch acres with every felling. The dryads take longer to emerge if there are too many cuttings in the same area. It's better to keep switching places. No one's stolen onto our property to cut more trees, but who's to say if next week doesn't bring more loggers.

"You can't run with that arm." Dad's words are clipped. There's no room for discussion.

"I know." Craig sighs. "Beth can run." Finally he looks away from the forest and nods at me. "She's fast and she's always wanted to. She's been out here as long as I have, she's paid her dues."

"No." It's quick, decisive. "She can't."

I'm not surprised by my father's reaction. It doesn't matter that I've followed them since my childhood or that I've trained longer. There are no children to distract or slow me down. I can run but they've never let me. It's never been an option.

"Beth?" Craig asks. "Do you want to run? If dad binds my arm, I can keep lookout."

"Yes." There's a grin spreading across my face. I want to run. I've always wanted to run. At home, I keep to the street. Hard stone beneath my feet keeps me focused. It's easy to know your limits when the path has already been set and marked. In the forest there's no limits, no guidance. Even just standing amid the trees, my old life strips away. I have never craved anything the way I crave the sound of rustling trees.

Dad sits on the fallen oak, weight forward on his bad knees until the cartilage pops. He frowns, "I don't like it. She's never run before, it's too dangerous."

"I can do it." It's like being a child again, begging to join them. Pleading to just try on Craig's costume and promising that I wouldn't dare run in it.

"Beth ... do you still hear the sound?" Dad asks it softly, hesitantly.

The hum is always there. I feel it every time I'm near a tree. It's gentle, like the whooshing of blood through veins. The steady pulse of the world around me. The sound is stronger when the dryads emerge, it becomes dizzying and intoxicating. It's why I have to live in the city, limiting my time in the woods to these few outings. Gray buildings, busy roads, they have their own sounds. Loud, of course. Everything in the city is loud. But it dampens the call.

"I haven't heard it in years." The lie comes so easily. It falls off the tongue without thought, without hesitation. For a moment, I almost believe it, too. "Not since I was little."

Dad trusts me. I can see it in his face. He's wary and concerned about the danger, but he has no reference to double-check. Mom and grandma are not with us in the woods. There's no other woman to ask for the truth.

I asked my grandmother about the noise when I was little. I hated being left behind to watch as my brother got to become a god for an afternoon. She told me that when she was little, she had been the runner once. Her brothers had all gone off to fight and she was left behind to help her father with the farm. She wore her brother's deerskin suit and spent a month practicing darting through the forest. When she blew the whistle, another sound triggered, a hum from the forest that she felt down to her toes. She ran and never wanted to stop. She ran and ran, luring the dryad deeper into the trees—until she swore that both she and the dryad forgot about the old oak tree, until she wanted to disappear into the hum of the forest. Since then, we've been left to wait on the sidelines.

When dad brings up the story, it's easy to remind him that it all happened fifty years ago, two generations removed. He doesn't like it, but Craig's confidence sways him.

Craig hands me the bone flute. When I was little, the carvings entranced me. I'd always hold it carefully on the drive out to the woods, making sure it didn't jostle as we drove over rocks and stumps. It's shaped like a pan flute, made with hollowed bones. Mom used to say they were just chicken bones, but I've never seen a bird with bones that shape.

I stoop a little, so Craig can paint the gold on my nose, taking care to swipe it across my cheeks. The paint dries quickly and crinkles softly when I smile at him.

He surprises me by dipping in for a quick hug. It's sudden and awkward. Craig mutters something under his breath. It sounds like an apology but the words are lost before he pulls away.

"Ready?" Dad shouts. The chain saw is by his hand, ready to be grabbed once I'm past the first marker. Craig has scrambled on top of the carriage bed so he can see how far into the forest I go.

My teeth clench on the flute, its leather tie stretched against the back of my neck. I breathe through my nose, careful not to make a sound too early. This time when the whistle blows, it echoes from my lips to my ear drums, louder than anything I've imagined. This close, it drowns out the sound of heartbeats in my ear.

The first marker blurs behind me before I even realize that I started running. There's no ache in my legs or chest. Any initial awkwardness melts away as my strides lengthen and pace increases. I blow the whistle again to keep the dryad's attention. When the grind of the chain saw starts, I know for sure that the dryad is giving chase.

The branches reach out, their limbs rubbing against my own. My arm burns from their scratches, I don't know whether to veer into them to get a deeper cut or avoid them completely. The thrum of the forest has caught up, drowning out the chain saw. She's behind me but I can't say how close.

The buzzing continues until my vision doubles. The chain saw is somewhere far beyond me. I can't see the orange markers meant to guide the runner, telling them how far they are from camp. If I've passed them, I've run too far already. Losing track of sightlines is dangerous. There's always the chance the dryad will abandon the chase in order protect her home. Still something tells me to run, and run, and run. My neck prickles, my coat is damp from sweat that drips from my forehead and burns my eyes.

Grandma used to say our family carried a light inside of us; it just glowed a little more brightly in me and her. At night, when the men were still out in the bush, she'd tuck me into bed and tell me stories about her mother, the fair maiden her father found in the woods. It was why we belonged out there, she'd say. Why we could hear the heartbeat of the forest until it flowed in our veins like sap through the trees. It was dangerous to get lost in it.

Everything blurs. All I can hear is the forest; all I can see is an endless path that just takes me further away from the song. Maybe I can outrun the sound, run until I reach the clearing, leave that buzz somewhere far beyond me. I don't think I can. The music is intimate and natural. It feels more like home than the city ever has.

I stop running.

In that loss of momentum all of my body's aches came to the fore. The muscles in my legs stretch and pull like saltwater taffy. There's a stabbing stitch in my side. It'd all disappear if I started running again. I know it to be as true as my grandmother's stories. It takes a few blinks before my vision clears. There are no markers. I can't tell if I've run in a straight line. Nothing looks familiar. There's the dim roar of a chain saw that sounds like it is miles away.

The forest hums at a higher pitch. I can almost hear a song lost in the tones. The dryad is behind me but the music doesn't sound like a warning. Her scent is carried by breeze, sharp like pine but heady with decay. It's earth and life, rot and death. Strange and unsettling, but completely familiar. It feels like reaching the end of a race that I didn't know I had been running.

The dryad moves in front of me. Her wisp is small, no larger than a fist, but it radiates light so it seems larger. Dad would call the color green but he's never seen them properly. There's too much brown and red. The wisp brightens until there's a brief shadow of a woman. But the shape disappears when my eyes readjust. The forest's pulse skips a beat.

The wisp shakes until the trees shake with her. The ground is still, the birds don't move, but I can see the trunks of the trees rattle back and forth. I could start running, I should. The dryad hasn't caught me, not yet. But she's so close and my family seems so far away.

Had Craig been lured by the sound too? Had he felt the same compulsion to stay? My brother and I so rarely find common ground. These trips to the woods are all there is between us. Once dad goes and Craig brings his children instead, we won't even have that.

The wisp gets closer and everything becomes simple.

The pounding in my blood, echoing the call of the forest. A tree falls, or we do. That's always been the trade when felling trees. There's the human urge to flinch and flee, but it's buried under the dryad's song. My skin buzzes when the light touches it. The dryad song changes, it twists until it matches my pulse. It's like remembering a lullaby, one that you only heard as a child but remember just the same.

"What are you doing to me?" My ears are ringing, my nose bleeding. Is this what happens to the other hunters? My hands are shaking, but I notice a faint green glow under my fingernails. There's the bright blue of my veins underneath the light.

"You've felt the call and are retaking the form that was denied to you." There's no voice. But the words are heard. "Your people have taken our homes. Those who don't steal from us, kill us while we're sleeping."

I think of the dead oaks stained with red sap. The small acorns that drop to the forest floor and take root. Each tree has its own song that continues even when the dryad loses her home and makes another. My father and brother have never seen them, never heard their song. Disappeared is a good enough word for them, dead is even better.

"We rejoin the leaves until we create a home again." The wisp answers what I don't ask. "Hundred of years."

The blood from my nose tastes thick and sweet, like sap.

"Once your family took one of ours. We've waited a long time for one of our own to return. Your brother promised that you would join us."

My legs are rooted to the ground. They feel heavy and stiff. The forest has never been clearer, the songs sharper. "Craig?" There's no surprise. His reluctance to touch me, his willingness to send me as a runner, his mumbled apologies.

The dryad blinks, her color fading. It takes a moment to realize that, beneath the forest's noise, the chain saw has stopped. The tree is down, her home is gone. She's disappearing. My father will be hacking at the strip of bark still tying the tree to the base.

There's a frisson running through my body, one I'm tired of ignoring. My skin burns and glows as it changes. It reminds me of the brightness of my clock back home. I've spent years staying awake and watching those numbers. Waiting for the moment I could go outside and run again. I craved grass and trees but was willing to settle for gravel and building.

I called my grandmother weak for avoiding the forests. Thought that she was too afraid, too old-fashioned, too fixated on her family. She had run faster and harder than I could. She outran the dryad, outran the forest's call. Her single-mindedness drove her. She wanted home and family. I never cared for either.

If I close my eyes I can see him and my brother. One waiting for me to return, the other hoping that I don't. There's no room for anger in my changing. The jealousy that spiked whenever he slathered on gold paint and started running seems distant and petty. I'll join the forest floor and grow into my roots.

We'll both age, we'll both die. But I will grow tall and he will shrink back into the earth.

■

Rebecca writes speculative fiction with small town flair. She's based in Canada's capital and spends her free time as a friendly neighbourhood Associate Editor at Apparition Lit. Her short stories and poetry have been published in Strange Horizons, Devilfish Review, Bewildering Stories, Non Binary Review *and* Flash Fiction Magazine. *You can follow her occasional tweets at @_rebeccab*

IN-CASE-OF-FIRE SHELF

■

Nicholas Siegel

A friend once told me she had a shelf in her living room dedicated to the books she would quickly grab in case of a house fire. These, she explained, were mainly first editions, signed copies, or old sentimental books from her childhood. One I remember was a copy of *Green Eggs and Ham* her mom had written a note in: "Read this and think of me when I can't be with you."

This gave me the idea to make my own in-case-of-fire shelf. Instead of just books, though, I wanted to stay more open-minded. My shelf would be for *anything* I wanted to quickly grab during a fire. I thought picking its contents would be easy—that the items so precious to me would call out like a vocation. This list was the best I could do.

YOUR HEART

It would go directly in the center of the shelf. If a fire were to break out, I would grab your heart, dripping with blood, and shove it into the stomach pouch of my hoodie or my pants pocket or the pocket of my jacket, the fat slick against my fingers. I'd be careful not to grip too tightly—to not accidentally squeeze and pop the delicate organ, although I've heard the thick blood from a popped heart can protect against natural disasters. That's not the point. That's not why it's on the shelf. It's on the shelf because there was a time when it was the only thing that made me happy. There was a time when it would have been the only thing on the shelf.

A FRAMED PICTURE OF MY BORDER COLLIE

When I was a kid, my sister and I had a border collie named Alex. Alex liked to go outside during thunderstorms. Before we adopted him, I'd never heard of a dog who enjoyed thunderstorms, but dogs' personalities are as varied as our own—this I know with certainty. One day we were all coming in from a storm after church, and Alex shot under our legs and out the door. My dad chased after him for a while, but the rain was coming down so heavily it was difficult to see. He told us we'd go looking again when the storm was over. I said when the storm was over, Alex would come home anyway.

The picture is from when he was a puppy, since he never did come back, and we didn't have any good pictures of him as an adult. It's in a gold frame with a thick chip in the bottom right corner. I still look for him sometimes when it rains.

A MASON JAR FILLED WITH SAND

The Mason jar itself isn't special, but the sand, from a beach on the Panhandle of Florida, was collected on the day I first saw an animal I didn't recognize. It was one of those summer days when the sun reflected so brightly off the sand I couldn't keep my eyes fully open. I waded out into the water until it was up to my waist and swam against the waves. Dark patches of seaweed floated around me—harmless shadows just under the surface. One of these shadows, however, brushed up against me, expertly weaving its way between my legs. It was slick like your heart.

I stroked backward so I could get a better look, and the thing came close to the surface of the water. I'd never seen anything like it. I didn't call anyone to me. I didn't look it up later. I tried to consciously forget the details of its anatomy, like I had to forget the details of yours. I wanted there to be things I didn't know.

In the days after Alex ran away, my sister and I would stay up late and talk about animals—about if there were still animals out there that no one had ever seen. I want this to be true so desperately it hurts.

THE FIRST SONG I EVER WROTE ON A WHITE CASSETTE

You spend your life listening to music, and then you make music, and it feels like you've broken into the dark gear rooms of the universe and fucked around with the machinery. I wrote this song in high school on an acoustic guitar with heavy gauge strings. I rehearsed it so many times my fingers bled, and I left the blood stains on the front of the guitar because I thought it looked cool. The song was about how the world is fundamentally different when it's stormy out. About how everything shifts a little to the left, just barely—almost imperceptibly. About how once this shift happens, you can look at people you love or places you know and hardly recognize them. Then, once the weather clears up, there is a light vibration and everything clicks back into place like a twisted throat muscle righting itself.

I recorded it on a Panasonic boombox, and you can hear the sound of my cat knocking things over in the background. I've always meant to go back and listen to it since I don't play anymore, but I'm scared it won't be quite as important as I remember, and I don't have anything that plays cassette tapes.

JANUARY 1996

Halfway into January, well past Epiphany, we still had our Christmas tree up. Most nights we joked about taking it down—that we'd get around to it eventually. Do you remember the night we originally planned to take it down? How we ordered Chinese and watched old Columbo reruns until about three in the morning when we both agreed it was an absurd time to take down a tree? How we plugged the tree in and set the lights to a slow blink before we went to bed? We wanted the neighbors to see it. We wanted them to know that sometimes Christmas can linger a little longer than usual.

Months are difficult to keep on shelves. They drip, and they don't stay in Mason jars like sand does. You have to think about months—to make sure you don't forget the little details, and the longer they stay there the worse they get, like food spoiling. You have to water them like plants, just not with water.

This is why I'm only saving this one for if a fire breaks out. I've had a lot of good months, and I've had a lot of bad months, but when and if I have to start over, having this one will be enough.

An unsmoked Pall Mall

One Halloween during college, I went with a group of friends to a rock concert at a hole in the wall venue downtown. The headliner, Ebony Lung, was why I wanted to write music in the first place. I had all their records, most of which were worn down. I had the pops and hisses on every track memorized.

I drank too much, and so did my friends. Once the show was over, we decided to wait outside just in case the band showed up. The sky had that faint green tint to it that sometimes precedes tornadoes. When the band finally came, we all talked and drank more. Jon, the lead vocalist, offered me a cigarette. I didn't smoke, but I didn't want to turn down the offer, so I took it, thanked him, and tucked it behind my ear. He glanced at it for a moment but didn't ask why I wasn't smoking it. His eyes were the same shade of green as the sky, like he had two holes in his head.

That night, before I got in the shower, I realized I still had the cigarette behind my ear and brushed it out. I was so drunk and tired, I didn't think twice about it, but the next morning when I saw it on the floor by the air vent, I knew I'd always keep it.

MY FIRST MOTORCYCLE

If it weren't for the crash, I'm not sure I'd want this one for the shelf. It was right after we met, remember? I was going to meet my friend David at his place, and all the lights on the highway were out. The weird thing about that was I made it down the highway fine. I actually crashed in David's neighborhood—right into a tree five houses down.

It happened in a flash like they always say it does. I was driving down the street, and then a split second later I was completely still, watching smoke rise from the front of the bike and drift up into the branches. There was a bird in the tree when it happened, and even though the crash didn't scare it off, the smoke did.

I didn't stop riding bikes after that like I should have, but I never got rid of or had that first bike repaired. I felt a bad energy in it. Something that has that type of energy is important. You don't just throw it away.

A LETTER FROM MY FIRST GIRLFRIEND

If you look closely at the paper, you can see where she started to write it in pencil, erased everything, and started over in pen. I've tried to decipher what it was she'd originally written. I've held it up to the light and looked through a magnifying glass at every possible angle—she did a great job of erasing it. I'm less interested in what the letter actually says than what it originally said, but in some weird way, it's all still there.

That had been a real train wreck of a relationship. It only lasted a few months, but we liked to stay up late planning what our life together would be like—who we'd invite to the wedding, what we'd name our kids, whether or not we'd live in a new house or an old one, what type of pets we'd get.

Eventually, I grew distant. I'd make excuses to not have to see her—anything I could think of. When I couldn't make up excuses anymore, I told her I needed to spend some time away with my friend in Nashville. I packed up, told my parents I'd be gone for a while, and disappeared. That's when she wrote the letter. It was her way of breaking up with me, even though she never explicitly stated it in what she written. I'd never felt more manipulative. I made her do the dirty work for me, and I was free.

It stays on the shelf as a trophy. It reminds me that everyone has a breaking point, and if you push hard enough for long enough, you can break anyone.

A BLACK ROSARY IN A SMALL, LEATHER POUCH

For many years, I worked at a record store. My manager saw the pouch, covered in muddy footprints, one day on the floor in the bluegrass section. For weeks, it sat under the register.

When I saw it and asked who it belonged to, she told me about finding it there on the floor—about how her first instinct was to throw it in the trash, but when she pinched the pouch open and saw the light glimmer off the cross, she thought maybe tossing it would be bad karma.

THE BIRD FROM THE TREE I CRASHED INTO

I think it was a sparrow of some kind—I've never been good at identifying birds. I always wonder how a bird would be relaxed enough to stay in a tree after the impact of a motorcycle—the initial shock, the vibration, the falling leaves. Although it could have flown down after the crash; I only saw it sitting there once the realization set in that I was no longer moving down the road.

And then the smoke. That's all it took for the bird to fly off, like it was rude for me to have polluted its resting spot with fumes. It was all I could focus on as it flew off into the sky, growing smaller and smaller until the expanse of blue subtly swallowed it whole. I wanted to watch the bird because I was afraid if I looked down, I would see that a leg was missing or that I had a gash in my side with organs spilling out into the grass. When I did look down, I saw that I was fine. The next day I had some bruises, but I was fine.

It must have taken some real courage for that bird to stay where it was—to decide that even though its home was literally shaking, it would rather wait it out until things got worse.

There's a nail in the side of the bookshelf, and hanging from it is a burlap sack. I figure I can pretty quickly slide everything into the sack and then make my escape out the front door like some weird Santa Claus with a backdrop of flames. The month will make it heavy, and I'll have to leave enough of an opening for the bird to get air. Your heart will pulsate in my pocket reminding me why all this is worth saving in the first place.

And all that's left, at this point, is to wait for the fire.

■

Nicholas Siegel is a writer from Louisville, KY who holds his MFA in creative writing from Spalding University. His fiction has been published in 7x7 LA, Palooka, *and* Jersey Devil Press, *among other places. He is a lover a bourbon, coffee, music, and cats. You can find his work at nswriter.com.*

WHITE NOISE

— ■ —

Gretchen Tessmer

On her knees in a dark, coniferous forest, Mei-Lin Kensington tries to think. Her head is buzzing with white noise. She tries to piece together fragmented thoughts but her mind is hazy, muddled and half-cluttered. When she tries to focus, she can imagine a rainy, ruined tower and her father's ... wait, a black hole, with flickering violet ... now slate clouds, little strips of ... no, it's no good. A rainy, ruined tower.

And her name is Mei-Lin Kensington, she knows that. There are solid edges to that thought, but the clumsy fingers in her mind can't reach them, already it tumbles, slips and slides like a glass of water spilling off a table. She stares at the mud-smeared knees of her journeyman's trousers and the linen sleeves of her tunic, stark white against the rust red of her bloody hands. Blood? She spins her upper body around, muscles tensing.

The first thing she sees is the door. There's no missing it. It's a door in the middle of a forest. A red door with white molding and thick hardwood planks. The door isn't attached to anything. The forest clears on either side of its high-reaching planks. The door's brass doorknob stares her down. Uneasy, she looks away from it and surveys the rest of her surroundings more fully.

The woods are dusky and dim, all knotted grays and greens, with one wisp of orange light drifting down through a thick canopy above, illuminating the forest eerily. The whole landscape resembles underwater depths, with an uncanny stillness. There's an absence of breeze and no scurrying and scampering of forest creatures. The forest floor is littered with brown and decaying pine needles, and the lowest branches of the conifers are all bare, gray and skeletal. Beside the door, the wispy orange light glints off a shallow pond of still water.

Crawling to her feet, Mei-Lin strides to the pond immediately, kneeling at the edge and thrusting her bloody hands into the murky water. In her haste, the wrists of both her sleeves are soaked. Long, loose strands of her black hair fall into her eyes but she neglects to push them away.

She scrubs her hands clean manically, using mud from the pond's edge mixed with fallen needles from the bank. The blood washes away easily, freshly shed and not her own. Her hands are unscathed. She calms a little, her breath coming more evenly. She sits back on the bank and again, tries to focus.

She whispers to herself, "Left to Ellsway, right to elsewhere." She grimaces, not knowing what her own nonsense means and concerned that the two-line mantra is a sure sign of madness. And that's when she hears a sound, the first sound in these quiet, dense woods. A bird's call, soft and carefully mimicked. It doesn't repeat her words but the same cadence is cooed out in eight syllables. The mockingbird gives the sounds a pathetic quality that Mei-Lin finds fiercely irritating. She glances up in the direction of the noise and glimpses white plumage on the upper doorframe and gray feet tightly gripping the white edge of the coarsely fashioned wood molding.

The bird stares at her, head cocked, and coos again. With a frown, she finds a rock in the undergrowth and throws it at the upper frame, hoping to scare it off. It's the small victories. The mockingbird flies off with a shrill call of protest in its own scratchy, undeveloped voice.

Mei-Lin rocks back on her heels, her eyes now settled and brooding over the structure before her. She may not know where she is or what she's doing here, but she can guess where she came from. And she bets anything that it's on the opposite side of that door.

"She cut me!" Carter keeps grabbing at his shoulder as Matilda tries to mend it. She slaps his hand away.

"Leave it alone! I have to sew it up ... unless you want a scar running the length of your shoulder?" Matilda asks slyly. That shuts him up.

Carter is a vain man and too proud of his appearance. With his tall, elegant stature, pleasing features and thick mane of blue-and-coal-black hair, there's no reason he shouldn't be. By comparison, Matilda is short, plump and past her prime. Time has cured her of all vanities. She has no regrets.

She stands on a three-legged stool threading a needle with thick black thread and looks ridiculous next to her tall, handsome son, she has no doubt. But there's no one else present to see them, so what's it matter?

They stand in what was once the old kitchen of a lauded manor house. The ownership of the house has recently changed hands and it's fallen into disrepair in an awful hurry. The once-cheery kitchen now resembles a dungeon, with a fireplace ablaze at one end, steam rising from black pots hung over it, a stone staircase at the other, twirling up and out of the darkness past moldy rafters and old, crumbling pillars. A long trestle table is set up in front of the fire, a bowl of herbs upon it and cages filled with bats and rodents beneath. The bats flutter their wings in the firelight. The mice scurry in the hay-strewn cages.

The room is long and arranged on three different stone levels, leading up to a massive iron door at its center. There are no windows in the room and the light from the fire's glow flickers unevenly throughout, casting shadows everywhere.

"Next time, don't run after her and maybe you'll have better luck catching her." Matilda bites off the excess thread with her teeth.

"Mother, that door leads to any number of places. There won't be a next time. She's gone." Carter turns his head, grabbing his shoulder and pulling the skin toward him to get a better look at the stitches. They are neatly done but bloody and too black against his skin. Matilda swats his hand away once more.

"Do you want to pull the stitches out!" she bellows. He releases his arm immediately and she hops off her perch onto the stone floor. "Sometimes you can be as stupid as your father, you know that?"

Her footsteps echo across the dais as she approaches the iron door on the other side of the room. Using the carved lion's head door knocker, she pounds twice. The sound of iron striking iron resonates throughout the room. The door opens a crack, scraping loudly against the stone floor, and a silver-haired man peeks his head out. A violet-colored birthmark in the shape of a roughly drawn gosling covers half his face. His hair is long, stringy and drenched. Rain is falling steadily on the other side of the door.

"Yes, Matilda?" he asks, without opening the door any wider. He sneezes once.

"Carter's lost the girl again," she says flatly. "Did she pass your way by chance?"

"No, ma'am," the man answers, pulling a checkered handkerchief out of his breast pocket before sneezing again. "Haven't seen anyone in the Ellsway for a good long time. Not since you pushed Cain Kensington out the sky door. He was the last one. But I've been watching ... day and night, like you said. Even though it's been raining night and—"

"I hope so," Matilda raises one eyebrow ever so slightly. "That's what I'm paying you for." The silver-haired man mumbles something about his last paycheck or lack thereof. He blows his nose into the handkerchief, loudly.

"Well, go on then!" she shoos him out, ignoring his complaints. "Go earn your wages. And if that girl comes through your door, you keep her close and bring her here immediately, do you understand?"

"Yes, ma'am," the man ducks his head subserviently before pulling the door closed. Thunder rumbles as the lock clicks shut. Carter grabs a white shirt from a brass hook on the wall and pulls it on without washing his arm. Blood seeps through like wine spilled on a white tablecloth. Still infuriated and indignant, he doesn't notice.

"How do you know she'll go back through the door?" he demands. "What's to stop her from taking off in any direction? There are two thousand doors. She could have come out on the side of any one of them."

"If you were faced with an unknown landscape or a door, which would you choose, my son?" Matilda asks patiently, arms across her ample chest.

"I wouldn't choose the door," he answers petulantly. He resents his mother's patronizing terms of endearment. He's nearly 30 years old. His opinion deserves some measure of respect. "Not if I'd just come through it."

"But that's because you *know* what's on the other side," she replies. "That girl doesn't remember anything, not even her own name."

"For now ...," Carter pouts, noticing the blood on his clean shirt at last. "And what happens when she does remember?"

"She won't," Matilda uncrosses her arms and walks to the fireplace and trestle table, to her boiling pots and caged animals. "She'll be dead long before she remembers anything. Because you'll kill her beforehand just like I killed her father"—she picks up a small paring knife and points it back at him for emphasis—"or you'll spend the rest of your life on the other side of that door as well."

"Mother!" Carter protests, looking up from his spoiled shirt only briefly. He whines, "You wouldn't do it."

"Just one turn of the lock, my son," she speaks slowly, dragging a rat out by its tail and slitting its throat in a swift motion. The beast bleeds out into a waiting tea cup. Her thumbnail is scarlet. She looks up at Carter, who stares at her warily.

"You're still here? Well, I'll give you to the count of five ..."

Mei-Lin stands motionless before the door in the woods. The mockingbird has returned but remains quiet, as quiet as Mei-Lin, breath even and her eyes alert. That orange wisp of light wraps itself around the water of the pond beside her. The red door beckons. She feels drawn to it. She knows she should open the door.

Her hand stretches out and touches the cold doorknob, heavy, metallic, brass. Her fingers slide around its neck and her wrist tilts slightly, rightward. The mechanism clicks and she imagines a humming. With one strong pull, it will be open ... again? *This is right,* she thinks. *This is what I'm supposed to do. Yes?*

The mockingbird begins cooing, pitifully. The bothersome bird is mocking her soul now. She glances up at the dowdy creature with a set frown. It stares at her before shuffling its feet slightly and turning its head away from her. With its tail feathers hanging over the door frame, the bird releases its bowels on her outstretched hand.

"Really? You son of a—" Mei-Lin slams the door shut with her palm flat on the planks. The mockingbird nearly laughs, an inhuman laugh, a sound learned from hyenas or vultures in the forest, and flies off deeper into the green woods. Mei-Lin flicks the white junk off her hand and, in a rage, runs after it.

• • •

"But why didn't you write?" Angelica looks at Carter plaintively, but stronger accusations are forthcoming. She mutters, "You could have written."

Carter sighs. With infinite doors to infinite places ... he ends up in the Hamptons. Of course he does. With Angelica waiting for him. The doors apparently have a sense of humor. The slight girl clings to him, tossing her copper-penny hair with a flirtatious flip. Her hair smells like peaches and passion fruit but Carter has no time for this. He slips out of her clinging arms and shrugs her off.

"Angelica, listen ... how about I make it up to you? Let me take you out to dinner? Tomorrow night?"

"Carter, I'm not stupid," she adopts a petulant expression. "You said that last time and I got all dressed up and you never showed—"

"Yes, but I was lying last time," Carter points out. "This time it's for real. You and me, babe. What d'you say?"

Angelica's pout lessens as she searches Carter's face for any indication that he's being insincere. She blinks her dark brown doe eyes once before smiling prettily. Throwing her arms around his neck, she covers his face in a flutter of butterfly kisses, "Oh, Carter! Yes of course. I'll buy a new dress. We'll be so beautiful together. The envy of everyone!"

"Yes, we will," Carter nods his head violently while disentangling himself from her octopus-like grasp. He gives her a couple more million-dollar smiles and says, "In fact, you should go get that new dress right now. Put it on my card. Leave Daddy's at home this time. Treat yourself to something nice."

"Oh, I should, shouldn't I? There isn't much time." She kisses his lips once more before leaving, blowing a parting kiss to him with a joyously tearful "I love you, Carter" spoken through trembling lips.

"Love ya too, babe," Carter gives her a thumbs up. She smiles, he smiles.

As soon as Angelica turns the corner, Carter wipes the grin off his face and steps back through the nice, clean linen closet door he had stepped out of no more than five minutes before.

Right to elsewhere, left to the Ellsway. Mei-Lin stops short. The woods seem to slow around her. The trees, which have been rushing past her at a breakneck pace, stand still, moaning and creaking in old age and the smallest change of weather. The mockingbird flies off without her. Immediately and obsessively, she presses her free hands to her pockets, pants, shirt, brushing past her chest only in the process. *There it is*. Hanging around her neck on a short chain. With a sharp pull, she yanks the chain free. A bronze key is clutched in her right hand.

But why—

"Oh!" she cries aloud and rushes back the way she came.

"So there I was, with a pistol in one hand and a hostage in the other and you know what he says to me?" Barnabas could talk a barnacle off an ocean tanker. And Carter is running behind. He waits for the man to answer his own question, twirling his hand to motivate Barnabas to be quick about it. They're standing on the eastern dock of Picacheque Bay in the Borderlands. It's quitting time. The silver sea is calm all the way to the horizon and dinner won't be for another two hours. The short sailor twists his full mustache and takes his time.

"He says, 'Do your worst.' It was the most ridiculous thing I've ever heard. I mean the hostage was all crying quarts and acting the part, but *this* guy. 'Do your worst.' Probably straight out of a drugstore penny dreadful. He's the type to throw good cash money away. I couldn't believe it. So I laughed and shot a cuff link off his shiny new suit and then pushed the hostage in the Bay. He went right in after the kid, headfirst, new suit, cowboy boots and all. Probably would've saved him too, except those ol' grinning croc-whales were out and you know how—"

"Yes, sounds tragic," Carter responds politely, before repeating himself. "Now you're sure you didn't see a girl pass by here? It wouldn't have been more than an hour ago your time."

"Nope, no girly through here. I would've remembered that." Barnabas winks solicitously. Carter waves him off. Blood-orange crab fish, with a dozen legs a piece, jump up and down in the silver water.

"Not that kind of girl. I'm looking for a bounty hunter's daughter. The half-and-half. Mei-Lin, you remember?"

"Sure, she's a spitfire. That whole family's full of spit and fire. What'd you do, lose her?"

"Something like that."

"Well that's no good. I'd hate to think how your mother would run her business having to travel between worlds the old-fashioned way. And that girl knows which door needs to be locked to lock them all, doesn't she?"

"Not anymore. Mother wiped her memory."

"You know those memory wipes don't last with the half-and-half. Too much Old blood in their veins."

"That's why I've got to find her fast."

"Well, at least she doesn't have the key, right? That would be a real disaster ..."

Carter doesn't answer, already down the dock, out the door and on his way.

In the Ellsway, it rains. In the ruins of a stone keep, the old man stands as close to the high stone wall as he can, attempting to escape the better part of the deluge and avoiding an otherworldly hole cut into the center of the tower and leading straight down to nowhere.

The early spring rain keeps pouring, with no notice to his discomfort. He sneezes at least twice every minute, leaning on his staff and pulling the sopping, checkered handkerchief from the pocket of his robes almost as soon as he stuffs it back in. This job isn't worth the pay. Especially since Matilda has stopped sending him checks.

The old man considers his options. With a face like his, the old man is not going to find honest work just anywhere. The grotesque, gosling-shaped birthmark takes up half his face. A hotel concierge, he is not. Not that Matilda's brand of employment is all that honest anyway. That whole business with Cain Kensington— well Kensington crossed a shady sorceress, what did he expect? Still, the whole thing feels hollow. Maybe he just needs a holiday. He hasn't taken one in fifteen years. He'll talk to Matilda about it once her mood improves.

The old man daydreams. He sneezes. Then he daydreams some more. Soon real dreams take their place. He falls asleep standing up, balanced against his staff and softly snoring.

For the first time in years, the black door across the keep opens.

Mei-Lin pulls the door closed from the rainy side of the Ellsway and locks it tightly. With a heavy sigh of relief, she sinks down against the door frame, worn out and way out of her element. She's a bounty hunter's daughter, sure. And her mother might be a fairy from the underworld beneath Hong Kong. It's all still a little muddled. Honestly, she found her way here by instinct more than anything else. Without the silly rhyme that is somehow written on the inside of her head, she would have turned the knob right, no question. So she'll take no credit for herself when she relates this story to others.

The keep is quiet, except for the constant drizzle of rain. The centerpiece of the sky tower spits a little back at the weather but mostly just stays still, its black-and-violet depths simmering sullenly. The high stone walls extend around the tower up, up, up. Other than the door she came through and the hole in the floor, there's no way out of the tower. Unless a person scaled the walls, maybe? Mei-Lin gives a brief glance up toward where the cinder-colored stones give way to the cinder-colored sky and casually wonders what lays beyond the walls of Matilda's favorite prison.

Matilda. The witch woman. The shady sorceress. Oh yes, I certainly remember her. Mei-Lin thinks, setting her lips in a firm line.

There's a silver-haired man standing directly across from her, leaning heavily on his knotted staff. He's obviously the sentry here, probably charged with orders to kill her upon sight, but he's currently asleep and seems harmless. Mei-Lin will deal with him if and when it becomes necessary. Not before. She's not the type to seek out a fight. Especially with an octogenarian plagued with sinus problems.

She lets herself rest for a good half hour, knowing that with the door locked, she's safe and sound for as long as she wants to be. But Mei-Lin's old enough to know that a safe life is no life at all. Besides, despite what that witch woman and her vain son believe, Mei-Lin didn't risk life and limb traveling to the Ellsway so that she could lock all the doors. They underestimate her ... and her family.

With her back still braced against the door, she reaches up and unlocks it. Then, with a flick of her wrist, she tosses the key in her hand across the stone floor of the keep. It clatters and skids across the wet floor to the open space in the center, where the sky door opens up to the shimmering, black-and-violet swirling nothingness below. The key slides off the edge and down into the portal like a penny falling into a fountain.

If she knows her father at all—and it's coming back in bits and pieces, flickers and flashes—he'll be waiting with open hands to receive it somewhere down below. Other people's revenge is a bounty hunter's bread and butter. But Mei-Lin has no doubt that his personal revenge will be a little sweeter and a lot more delicious than plain bread and butter.

While she waits, she turns introspective. Despite making it to the Ellsway in one piece, she thinks she might start carrying a pistol. But where to get one? Picacheque Bay maybe, though dealing with those obnoxious dock workers doesn't appeal to her. She'll ask the old man in the keep if he's got any ideas once he wakes up. She's willing to trade. She's got money to fix his face and she could recommend a good plastic surgeon in the Hamptons. She can't remember the doctor's name but he's good. His house has a nice, clean linen closet and he has a thoroughly vapid daughter named Angelica.

Oh yes, it's all coming back now.

The sky door starts spitting violet sparks. Mei-Lin reaches up and grasps the door knob above her. Someone's attempting to get in. She holds it fast, unafraid. In thirty seconds, the pursued and pursuer will abruptly switch places. The rattling door knob and the swirling, spitting sky door make quite a bit of noise, and the old man across from Mei-Lin wakes briefly. With sound judgment, he decides to ignore whatever is currently transpiring in the keep and lets himself drift back to sleep.

As soon as Cain Kensington emerges from the sky door, he takes one disapproving look at the slate clouds above him. Chastised, the rain in the Ellsway stops falling immediately.

Still sitting against the door, hands above her head, holding that door knob tight, Mei-Lin grins broadly.

■

Gretchen Tessmer is a writer/attorney based in the U.S./Canadian borderlands of Northern New York. She writes both short fiction and poetry, with work appearing in Nature, Strange Horizons, Daily Science Fiction *and* F&SF, *among other venues. For updates on her latest projects and publications, follow her on Twitter: @missginandtonic*

THESE ARE JUNO'S FIRST WORDS

---- ∎ ----

Saul Lemerond

I answer their questions as best I can, but half the time it's hard for me to remember my own name. My name is Jeff. They want me to tell them about my daughter. They always want me to tell them about my daughter. Juno. They also want me to tell them about the people who had kidnapped me before they did. It's hard to say. Everyone wears masks. All of them give me drugs, which messes with time. It's difficult to remember what happened before or after what. They all tell me this should be easy, that I should just tell them what happened in the order that it happened.

I don't know anymore what happened when. I really don't think it matters. I don't know if they want to kill my wife or if my wife wants to kill me, and I'm not sure why she would, and I tell them this, and they say they don't believe me.

I don't know if the Badgers got into the Final Four, and I don't know why I care because I don't like basketball. The drugs make it hard to put thoughts together, so I just give them whatever answer comes to me when they ask.

Sometimes they ask me questions that make me think about the person I was when I was a child. They ask, "What do you think your daughter was thinking?"

I answer them honestly. I tell them that when I was five, the only thing I cared about was dinosaurs, so I think that whatever she's thinking about probably has to do with dinosaurs. I tell them that my parents took me to see a movie that had them and after the movie, dinosaurs were all I could think about. I was always asking to go to the museum, and for books, and to look up things wherever I could. I tell them that's where she's at. It makes perfect sense. Kids love dinosaurs. Also, she insists on buttering her toast with a butcher's knife. It's one of her many eccentricities, but she hasn't cut herself yet and seems to know what she's doing. I tell them she could be considering alternative delivery methods of butter to toast.

The masks they wear and the questions they ask make me pretty sure other people in masks have asked me these same questions before. I tell them this. They seem very interested and want to know more. They want to know when. The drugs make this impossible. I do my best to tell them what I know about whenever it is they're asking. The drugs make everything distant. I tell them this. They do not care.

My phone rings all the time, same number, same sound of nothing on the other end. I tell my wife, Janet, that our daughter's speaking in websites.

"That's nice, I guess." she says, "She's growing up so fast. Eventually she'll be dead, just like everything else."

I tell her Juno misses her and that she should get out of bed.

"Has my father called?" she asks.

I tell her no because her father never calls, and I don't mention that she's treating our child the same way her father treats her.

Janet will only eat toast and drink cucumber water, and the old outline of her in the bed looks like a late day shadow because it's much bigger than she is now. The way she squints her eyes when she talks to me makes her look even smaller.

I bring our daughter, Juno, to Dr. Wu's office so she can tell me what she's saying. On this day there are more people than normal. There are four extra people. Two women and two men. No one in the office looks happy to see me, but they also don't look unhappy. They more look like static representations, like the office was put on pause right before we walked into the room.

Dr. Wu tells me they're here to help him with my daughter. That she's found an online domain that matches what my daughter's been saying.

"I wouldn't have been able to do it without them," she says, pointing at the others. "Please understand that I wouldn't have called unless I thought they could help."

Because I've stopped, their eyes stop following me, and they all look like a three-dimensional photograph again. My phone rings for the thirteenth time today, and I don't answer it.

"These two women, Johnson and Myers, are from the FBI," says Dr. Wu, motioning to his right. "These two, Smith and Kranz, are from the CIA," he motions to the two men to his left.

Johnson steps forward.

A loud bang comes from the reception area.

I don't remember closing the door, but I must have because it bursts open behind me, and several people, I cannot tell if they are women or men, enter the room with automatic rifles. They wear black winter coats, black work pants, black ski masks, and black reflective goggles. All of them have knifes, presumably they are not for buttering toast. We all put our hands up and do not speak. None of them speak, either. One holds up a picture of my daughter. One holds up a picture of me. Dr. Wu points to me and to my daughter. Then one of these people puts a blindfold over my eyes and holds a rag over my mouth and nose.

When they take our hoods off, they tell me that my wife has arranged for me and our daughter to be kept in a safe place. They tell me that everything will be fine. I just need to cooperate. I tell them I'd be happy to. They tell me they need me to speak to my daughter, and I tell them I wish I could, but there's actually no one who can do that. They tell me they're going to give me drugs. I say, great, also you might want to wait at the door for the next set of kidnappers to come because that's what always happens.

They shoot me full of something. There's a hood over my head so I don't see it, but at this point it doesn't really matter because it's all the same as before, and I tell them that. Just pass me off, I tell them. It's not like it matters. They could be anybody, really. It's possible they don't know my wife at all. They could be the same people I talked to before. They could be the people I talked to before that who also said my wife sent them, or maybe they're the first people I talked to. I wonder if I'm forgetting other times I've been kidnapped. I guess that's always a possibility. And they wonder why I have such a problem keeping track.

Janet's suffering from postpartum depression. Except, since our daughter's birth was seven years ago, it's probably safe to say she's suffering from just plain old melancholic-depression, and probably she always felt this way. Juno knows who her mother is. They don't talk. Our couples therapist tells me depression affects people in highly idiosyncratic ways. My wife's father calls us once a week to ask how his granddaughter is doing and to tell us he will once again be unable to visit on Christmas because he's made plans to go to Boca. I don't tell this to Janet.

I am blindfolded. I hear four gunshots. I assume four people are dead. I hope my daughter is also blindfolded and also not dead. They're going to move us again. I want to say something, but the last time I did someone hit me, and I woke up with a horrible pain in the back of my head and I didn't feel right for a couple of weeks. At least I'm assuming it was a couple of weeks. It's hard to know. I try to hold on to good memories, like the time when Juno pounded out in Morse Code that she loved me more than anything in the world.

Two and a half years into little Juno's life and she still isn't talking, though she pounds on whatever she can get her heels or fists on.

Whack, slam! Whack! Whack, slam!

It's 3 a.m.

Whack, slam! Whack! Slam!

I don't know what my daughter wants.

Whack, slam! Whack! Slam!

There is a part of me that wonders if my infant daughter is dying.

Whack, slam!...

Is she going to die or is she just hungry? Probably she's just hungry.

My wife, half awake, tells me not to worry. She mumbles, "Our universe is made up of equal parts of matter and antimatter, which means that all that 'is,' all that we know, can be expressed in a null equation. Everything 'is' minus nothing 'is.' Don't you see? The balance of everything equals indescribable absence."

I tell her that is simply not true.

She pauses for a moment, then says, "It's Morse code you know. She's hungry. She's pounding out, 'E, a, t.'"

I tell her that we should go to her.

"Has my father called?" she asks.

I tell her no and go feed our Juno. Once she's fed I cradle her in my arms and rock her back and forth until she sleeps.

We've moved again. This is not in doubt. I still think we're on State Street though, because I can hear someone who sounds like they're drunk yelling they are happy the University of Wisconsin's basketball team has won a game.

One of the agents takes off her scarf and mask and flashes her badge in my face, "You're here because we need you safe."

I ask from what

"Terrorists," she says.

The room we're in is dark and the windows are covered. I point to the window and tell them, "They had us in a dark room on State Street. You have me in a dark room on State Street. How is it that my daughter and I weren't safe there but are suddenly safe here?"

"We can keep you safe from them," she says, and takes out a syringe to give me more drugs.

"You moved us down the block," I say. "And they gave me drugs already, and why are you giving me drugs?"

"We've taken those terrorists into custody," she says. She points to the bottle she just used to fill up the syringe. "This is just something to help you relax."

I tell them I'm worried and that I'd like to see my daughter and talk to my wife.

"You have nothing to worry about," she tells me. "Your daughter is safe. She's in the other room. Your wife," she lets the word, "wife" hang in the air for quite a long time before she says, "Don't worry about her. We know what we're doing." She leans toward me so I can see her face in what little light there is. She has hard features. Satisfied features. Like she'd just cut off someone who'd cut her off a mile back down the road.

"Because you're from the NSA?" I ask.

"Yes," she says, "and we'll send you home just as soon it's safe." The room is empty except for chairs. There are exactly enough chairs for everyone to sit, though not everyone is sitting, probably it's those people's jobs to stand.

"We want to know," the agent says, "how your daughter knows quantum language."

"I don't know," I say because I don't. "Have you thought of asking her?"

The agent lets out a long sigh, and so do the rest of the agents. "We can't speak to your daughter. She's speaking in quantum. We don't speak quantum. No one does. The only way we know how she's speaking in quantum language is because we have people who think they know what it looks like."

One of the agents takes their knife from their belt and lays it on a table.

"That's unfortunate. I don't either." I say. "Have you thought of asking her grandfather? From what I understand, his company has been working on quantum computing for quite some time." I assume the drugs are working because I'm not supposed to be saying this and also because my body is vibrating with the frequency of several bee hives.

"You understand that your daughter, if she is speaking in quantum computer code, that that would make her the most dangerous person on the face of the planet?"

"Sure," I say, and realize she's referring to the only person on the planet I care about. I remember when she started speaking in html and made a beautiful website devoted to her and her dog, only she was the queen of the moon, and I was her loyal star dog.

• • •

The year after our daughter is born, there are weeks my wife does not leave our bed, and there are other weeks when she is fine. On her bad days, she lies under covers in a dark room, doesn't talk unless it is to ask after her father who never calls her, and is certain life has no meaning. On her good days, she goes to work where the entire physics department at UW basks in her brilliance as she works in tandem with Dr. Wu. Everyone she meets is impressed. When they ask if she has any children, she tells them that she has a daughter and that her name is Juno.

They make comments about our infant daughter. They say things like, "Her eyes are so brown. If your daughter has even half the intelligence you have," and then trail off in the way people do when they feel they don't have to finish their sentences. Every so often they ask what I do, and she tells them I teach economics online for the local technical college.

When our daughter Juno is one year old, she has yet to make a sound remotely resembling a word. Instead, she pounds on things. The whacks and slams echo through our substantial townhouse as I try to work in my study and Janet stares blankly at the TV in our dark room.

Lying under a thick down comforter with a Madison blizzard whiting out the view outside her window, she says, "It's okay. I don't want her to speak." Her phone is filled with messages from her TAs, and many of them from Dr. Wu, because she hasn't been to the University in weeks. She hasn't said/spoken more than two words to me in longer. Now she wants to talk about Juno, who is crawling in circles around the living room, and stopping every now and again to pick up blocks and pound them on things.

I ask Janet why she doesn't want our daughter to speak.

"Because," she says, "when she learns to speak she will ask us lots of questions and we'll have to answer them."

But she'd be talking, I say.

She points at the shadow the lamp casts of itself on the floor, "That shadow is a two-dimensional representation of a three-dimensional object."

The shadow looks like a very thin man in a funny hat.

"We're three-dimensional, Jeff. Three-dimensional objects give off two-dimensional shadows."

I don't ask her if she notices that, because she mostly never sees her, our daughter treats her in the same way she treats strangers, and I don't tell her that I happen to know how Juno acts around strangers in the park because I am the one who takes her there.

"There's a fourth dimension, Jeff. What do you think that makes us?"

I do not ask her if she thinks the reason she is depressed and doesn't engage with our daughter is because she's just reenacting all of the same mistakes her own father made.

"We're three-dimensional. This means that in four-dimensional space," she says, "we're just shadows. Does it make you feel good that we're probably just echoes, just impressions," she pauses trying to think of a better descriptive, and finally settles on, "just outlines of something far more complete? Is that something you want to tell our daughter or should I do it?"

I ask her if her dad ever talked to her about things like this when she was younger.

She says nothing, and leaves the room to go lay down. It's not surprising. She's never talked about her dad for as long as I've known her. She only asks if he's called.

It's spring, and Juno is four when she starts talking because she doesn't want to take a bath.

The sun's falling, and I tell her it's time for one.

She says, "0100111001101110."

Her voice is weak and light and squeaky, and rings to me like the opening bell of the stock market.

I ask her to repeat herself.

"0100111001101110," she answers.

I run into the office and write down the string of numbers fast as I can.

I go to my wife who is laying in the dark in our bed, read her the numbers, and ask her what it means.

"She doesn't want to take a bath," Janet says. "It's binary." She then spells out the zeros and ones, "'01001110': capital 'N'; '01101110': small 'o'."

I ask my wife why our daughter is speaking binary.

She shrugs and says, "If you want to understand our child, all that you need to do is learn ASCII. It's so simple an infant could learn it."

I look up ASCII and start to speak with my daughter in ones and zeros. I learn that my daughter sees the world is beautiful. I learn that she loves colors. I learn that she loves me and thinks her mother is sometimes sad and other times scary.

When my wife is feeling optimistic enough about life, she goes to work out equations with Dr. Wu, tells her co-workers I talk to our daughter in ASCII, and that her father is making great strides with research and development concerning quantum computing.

The other students and faculty are impressed. These are good days. The happy days. The days when she is out of bed, talking, working to advance all knowledge to limits previously unimagined. These days are not common.

The evening before my wife decides it would be a good idea to lie in bed for a year, I tell her at dinner how our daughter just told me in a large amount of ones and zeros that her new favorite color is bright pink.

My wife explains it can't be true, "There are an infinite number of wavelengths in the EM spectrum, and the amount of space between each color can be broken up into infinite sections and that any two possible points have an infinite number of points in between them. When Juno says she likes bright pink, she's saying she likes an infinite subset of an infinite number of possible colors, which isn't possible. We can't like infinite things, no matter how much we would like to." Janet rolls her eyes, "I think our daughter's entering her lying phase."

I do not respond. I do not ask her if it's true that her father was considered a person of interest by the police when her mother disappeared thirty years ago. I do not ask her if she remembers her mother. She's never once talked about it.

I stand in a room with five people who say they're from the NSA, though unlike the last group who kidnapped us, they've shown me no identification and have not taken off their goggles, masks, or coats. I'm in a dark room lit by only one small battery-powered lantern. I tell them I am happy to speak with them and do not need any drugs and perhaps they could provide me with their names.

They give me drugs, and do not give me their names.

"Can you tell us why your daughter has been in contact with nearly every single person of interest we have on file?" one of the agents asks.

I figure outside must be State Street because we haven't traveled far, and I can hear the howl of drunken college kids after a Badger game, though it's true the howl of drunken Madison kids is not exclusive to State Street.

"I don't know," I say, in the precarious position of having to assume these people are indeed from the NSA. "Maybe you should ask her. Also maybe you should let us go. I can't imagine any of what you're doing right now is legal."

"We're putting your wife on speaker," says one who might be the same one or might be one from before or might be a different one altogether. "When she answers, you are not to say anything unless we ask you a question, and in that case, you are only to answer it, nothing else." The person speaking pauses a moment to let this sink in, then asks, "Do you understand?"

"Yes," I say, though it's stupid they should imagine that I'd answer that sort of question any other way.

Janet doesn't answer the first time they call her. Nor does she answer the next dozen times.

"What do you want?" Janet sounds like she always does when she speaks, like she's exhausted and would rather not be talking.

"We have your daughter and we have your husband," one of the maybe NSA says. "If you want to see them again, you're going to have to answer some questions."

Janet doesn't reply.

Everything seems very far away.

"We want answers, and we want money. If you don't give us these things, we will kill your family. Is that clear, Ms. Janet?"

These people are not NSA agents. I look around for my daughter but cannot find her, but that's normal for both the kidnappings and my recent dreams. We've been kidnapped six times, or at least I think it's probably six, more or less.

"Time has no meaning," says Janet.

"We're serious," one of the masked kidnappers says, "When we say we'll kill your family."

It must have been cloudy, and those clouds must have parted because there's suddenly much more light in the room, and I'm wondering if these people are adolescents because they all look pretty short and thin to me. They remind me of a dream I have were Juno and I are kidnapped by terrorists and strapped with bomb vests and fired over the White House fence.

"We'll kill them. We'll kill your family. And we'll do it if you don't give us the answers we want and the money we want. Isn't that right, Jeff?"

Everyone in the room look at me. "Honey," I say, "these people are telling the truth. I think they might be terrorists."

"Sure," Janet says.

"Your daughter has intimate knowledge of our dark web activity. Where did she learn of this?"

"I'm not sure what you mean by intimate," Janet says.

"She has knowledge of things she shouldn't."

"I'm not sure what you mean by knowledge," Janet says.

"By knowledge, we mean that your daughter knows about where, when, and why certain factions in hidden locations are operating."

I'm reminded of a dream I have where Juno tells me she loves me so much she'll make a new world for me, and she does, and we fly through space to this beautiful new world that has rainbow skies, and when we get there we are kidnapped by people in black ski masks and voice modulators.

"I'm not sure what you mean by operating," says Janet.

"This is not a game, Janet. We know your daughter is smart, but she couldn't have known of these operations by herself. Did you turn her on to us?"

"Who is us?" Janet asks.

"Us is the terrorists."

"I'm not sure what you mean by terrorists," Janet says.

"You should know we are not playing games. We will kill your husband and your child."

There is a long pause.

"I understand why you would think this would concern me, but you'll have to understand that I'm not sure what death is, and I'm also very tired, and I don't think I can talk to you very much longer. I am very tired, and I'd like to go to sleep."

"We will kill your husband and your child. We demand you give us answers."

I'm reminded of a dream where Janet lifts us over her head, and while she's doing this, she's growing taller and taller, and I'm telling her she needs to spend more time with our child, and she's just growing bigger and bigger until we're right next to the moon and she sets us down and there's a house there and Janet says that she made this for me and Juno and that we should be happy here and I tell her thanks and she says she has to go, but not before we butter toast with sharp knifes. I like that dream. I always wake up wishing I was there.

"I don't have any answers," Janet says, "and I doubt anyone else does either."

"Then you will send us money, or we will kill your daughter and husband."

There is a long sigh on the other line that I have heard many times before.

The person who says they're an NSA agent and a terrorist cocks his rifle, ejecting a bullet that was already in his chamber. "That's the sound of the people you love about to die. I hope you're happy."

"I'm not," Janet says, and she hangs up the phone.

When my daughter is five, she says, "5EB52."

I tell my wife, who ignores me and replies that she would like a piece of buttered toast with honey, and asks me if her father has called.

I tell her no, and I get her buttered toast with honey. I dress Juno in a bright pink dress and take her out to the university.

When I bring my daughter to Dr. Wu, Juno says, "5EB52."

Dr. Wu's eyes light up. "It's hexadecimal," she says. She kneels down and excitedly looks into my five-year-old daughter's tiny autumn eyes.

Wu is a very serious woman and doesn't speak. She just watches and records Juno.

Wu shows her a red plastic box, and she says, "9E7TC." Dr. Wu writes this down. She shows her a multitude of other geometric shapes that are a multitude of different colors. She shows her pictures of animals living in sub-Saharan Africa. She shows her movies about bees in Ecuador that may no longer exist.

Sometimes Juno talks, sometimes she doesn't. Her listing of numbers and letters starts slow, and then continues to get longer. Wu watches doggedly, taking notes.

There are tears in my eyes because I'm wondering for the briefest of moments if these people are going to shoot me and my daughter like they said they would. But then the door bursts open and more people dressed in black who all have automatic assault rifles come in. My tears go away. Everyone is surprised and we all put our hands up.

"No one move," says one of the people dressed in a black long wool jacket and ski mask and reflective sunglasses. Their voices are also modulated.

One of the new people puts a hood over my head. They give me drugs to make me talk.

After three days, Wu tells me it's Hazni, the classic Chinese character group, that she's using hexadecimal code so she can speak Hanzi with less effort, "There are over ten thousand characters in Hanzi."

She says, "I showed her a yellow octagon. She said, 'This shape is round and bright like the sun. If it had more sides, and was more bright, it would be more like the sun. If it had fewer sides, and was less bright, it would be less like sun and more like a featureless shape.' When I asked her what she knew about the sun, she said, 'I have a lamp that lights my room. The sun is a lamp for all room.'"

Dr. Wu is silent for a moment, "Then she started speaking in html, and she's not making any sense."

I am thankful because my kidnappers are keeping my daughter in the same room as me for once. She has stopped speaking in letters and numbers, and now only screeches, which she does very seldom, which is good because the screeching is so high-pitched it can be painful at times.

"Your wife hired us to bring you here," is what these people tell me.

It doesn't make any sense because she doesn't care about anything. There is no reason why my wife would have us kidnapped. There are many days when I wonder if she even remembers that we, her husband and daughter, even exist. We've been gone for weeks, which means there's no one to bring her cucumber water or dry toast or toast with honey. She must have noticed that. This is not to say that she thinks we exist because that would be far too much to expect.

"Your wife knows that you two," starts that woman, or man, I can't tell because he or she is wearing a ski mask and is pointing one finger at each of us, "will fetch a lot of money." The woman or man stops for a moment and looks to the right, or I imagine that they look to the right because I can't tell which way they're looking because they're wearing googles. "Or at least one of you will. We're pretty sure it's the girl, but your wife wants you both, so that's that."

My daughter emits a screech for what feels like thirty very long seconds. At first we all cover our ears. But one of the kidnappers puts a rag over her mouth after a large crack appears in a windowpane that faces down into the busy street outside.

This doesn't appear to hurt Juno. She is, as far as I can tell, still screeching her mind. It's just that it's more muffled. I wish I knew what she was saying, but seeing as she's never really been comfortable around her mother, I imagine she's saying something about her mother being scary or dangerous.

"Does this mean you're going to take us back home," I ask. "Back to my wife?"

"No," the agent says. "We're going to keep you here until your wife can sell you to whoever bids the highest."

This is something I don't understand, and I tell them, "I don't get it." When they don't answer, I say, "Is she giving you a percentage?"

The agent looks at me for a moment. I have no way of telling what they are thinking. I can't see their face.

"No," the agent says. "Flat fee."

"That seems like a bad deal," I say. "I feel like you could probably do the same thing that she's doing and keep all of the profits. Plus, how do you even know it's her."

Juno's screeching gets higher. It gets louder and louder through the rag. She goes on. The agent with the rag over her mouth looks at the agent who is talking to me. No one seems to know what to do. Juno goes on some more, emitting a high screeching sound that reminds me of the sound I would get when I was a child and would want to use the phone, but I couldn't because my sister was on the internet, only it's as loud as a rocket launch.

One of the agents gets their phone out and starts recording. "This will be useful," they shout, and it's hard to hear them.

I look over to Juno, and she stops screeching just as soon as I open my mouth to speak. I have no idea why this is.

"Useful for what?" I ask, but I don't get an answer because, just as I finish my sentence, the door bursts open and a group of people burst into the room. They must have a battering ram because the door shatters into a million pieces as they enter. They wear all black, and their faces are covered with ski masks, and their eyes are covered with ski goggles, and their voices are disguised with voice modulators.

"You are coming with us," one of them says. "This is a matter of national security."

They put hoods over our heads, and Juno starts screeching again.

"Record that!" I hear one of the new kidnappers yell over the sound of my daughter.

• • •

When I first start dating my wife, I tell her that I used to be into guys. She says she doesn't care, and I take this to be a good thing but only later find out she doesn't care about anything. I wonder why she likes me. She tells me I am kind.

I don't ask her about her family. I know they must be well off because she looks very nice, which is to say that she looks very nice in a way that only a good deal of money can make a person look nice.

I am not wrong. Her family is in the business of making beer, or at least it was in the business of making beer. Now it's making beer and many, many other things. She is always very vague about it, like she's ashamed. But apparently they own a good part of the Milwaukee docks and over the years have gotten into politics and, in her words, "Everything that goes with that."

I meet her family one Thanksgiving. I'm nervous because Janet always talks about how important it is she make her father happy, and this makes me nervous. I sit at a dinner table as large as my first apartment and talk about my graduate school work. They all seem to be interested, even her father, and my soon-to-be wife later tells me that they all like me. Dinner goes well. I'm not sure I have any way to connect with a single member of this family, and I feel like they're judging me because I would judge me if I were them, especially if I were her father because I could never, ever offer her what he can.

When she is pregnant, she gets on the phone to tell her parents. She doesn't get to talk to her father, but she talks to her sister. She tells me the family is happy, and not just happy, but oh, so happy. I decided long before this that I would never let her ask them for anything. Not after the way her father treated her, still treats her.

After the phone call, when we're getting in bed to sleep, she asks me if I understand that the scientific method is irrefutably flawed.

I tell her that I'm not sure that it matters. At least not right now. Not with a baby on the way.

"It's important because I'm a scientist," she says. "The scientific method requires that all hypotheses be disprovable. That means that a scientist has to come up with one possibility that is disprovable. But the problem is that for any set of circumstances, there are actually an infinite amount of possible outcomes. If you disprove one outcome, you still have an infinite number of outcomes. If you work even harder and disprove orders more outcomes, that's great, but really, what have you done? There's always going to be an infinite number of outcomes you haven't disproven."

I tell her that I don't think that's right, that there are statistical probabilities.

"Please don't patronize me?" she asks, and stares at me for a long time.

Everything seems so distant. I try to remember Juno, and I know the name means something to me, someone who loves me and who I love, but everything's hard now.

I tell them no more drugs. I can't think good. They give me some anyway and take my hood off. Janet is standing there. In front of me. Not in bed.

"Why aren't you in bed? Did you suddenly find a reason to live in a universe that doesn't care about you?" The words come out, and I don't know why because I didn't make them.

"I like my bed," she says. "I want to stay in it. It's comfortable. Daddy says I can stay in my bed as long as I want if I get my daughter to just say what these nice gentlemen and ladies need her to say."

She motions at the people behind her who are wearing all black from head to toe.

"And those people?" I hear myself ask about the kidnappers who took me and Juno to the room we're in now.

"I asked them to bring you. But they don't need to be here right now," she says, "because this is a private conversation."

The agents look at Janet.

"Now," she says, and they abandon the room, leaving all of their equipment behind.

"Our daughter," she says, "is very smart, and she has the attention of the Pentagon because, they say, she can understand code at the level of a quantum computer. Do you know what a quantum computer is?"

I do, and I do not care. I see myself motion to our daughter, and hear myself saying, "She's right there. You don't need to talk about her like she's not in the room."

Juno starts screeching. It's a sound that I cannot describe. I can tell the frequency is changing. I don't know what she's saying, but I like it. Juno always speaks in ways I can't understand, but she always sounds like she loves me.

I hear multiple dogs start to howl. Juno stops screeching. She looks at me like she knows what I'm thinking.

"That's great," I hear myself say. "She's speaking in quantum." And then I see myself point to our daughter, gently, trying to let her know that even though I don't know what she's saying that I still love her and will do whatever I can to get her through this because I don't want her to feel any more pain because she doesn't deserve it. I wish I were closer. I wish I could be part of this.

"If she's speaking quantum," I hear myself say, "then that would mean it would take a quantum computer to decipher what she's saying. There are no quantum computers, which makes me wonder how anyone could know that."

"She can show us how to make one," my wife says. "We need her. She's the next step. We just need to figure out what she's saying."

Juno gets up and walks to her mother. I wonder how well she recognizes this person because she's only mostly ever seen her in her bed under her sheets explaining to the both of us that there isn't, and has never been, a good reason for anything.

"My father," Janet says. "This is what he wants."

"He wants to take our daughter," I hear myself say. I see Juno take something, some object, off the table.

"I'm his daughter, and he had me and wasn't that impressed, nor should he have been. Anyone can have a daughter. He wants quantum computing. I can't see a reason why he shouldn't have that."

I'm not sure, because it seems so far away, but as my wife talks it looks like Juno has a knife.

Juno then begins plunging the thing that I think could be a knife into her mother, and it must be a knife because there's so much blood, and my wife is screaming. Juno is screaming, too. But she's not really screaming so much as she is screeching. I can't tell what she's saying, but I can tell that she sounds like she loves me.

■

Originally from Green Bay, Wisconsin. Saul Lemerond lives in Madison, Indiana where he teaches creative writing at Hanover College. His work has appeared in Drabblecast, Dunesteef, *and elsewhere. He also has a book,* Kayfabe and Other Stories, *which is available on Amazon.com. You can find him on Twitter @SaulLemerond.*

SCRUBBED

■

Rich Larson

The waiting room is empty, but they sit together instinctively before they consider it might be better to be far apart. Each of them could have claimed for their own a dozen molded plastic seats, two chemical green walls, one glowing vending machine dispensing cold drinks and recyclable breath masks. Instead they are huddled together in the center of the room, and the fluorescent banks in the ceiling might as well be a spotlight.

The man is not quite a young man anymore. Mid-to-late twenties. He has a flat face, sunken eyes, the vestige of an expensive haircut unstyled and overgrown like his wiry beard. He wears acid yellow pants and a charcoal gray shirt opening two buttons deep on a sunburnt chest.

His expression is blank, his posture is relaxed, but one knee is pointed slightly inward, so his leg doesn't touch his companion's, and the lanky arm splayed along the back of the seat leaves a sliver of plastic between itself and his companion's shoulders.

The woman is older, late thirties. She has an angular face, sunken eyes, a small, pale mouth. When she opens it as if to speak, and then only breathes, a crooked tooth she never had fixed shows. There are flecks of black mascara on her cheek and flecks of silver in her short black hair. Her shirt has zippers that aren't designed to be pulled and tendrils of a tattoo reach across her collarbone. She sits very upright in her seat with her shoulders drawn back and then relaxed, a precise kind of posture compensating for an old dance injury. She leaves her bag on her feet, balanced centimeters over the dirty floor, instead of holding it in her lap.

The man turns his head so she knows he's looking at her, but his eyes don't actually fix on her face. They slide past to land on the wall, where the smartpaint mural—done back when it was a different sort of clinic—shows red balloons drifting across the green.

"If we have anything else to say, I guess this would be the time to say it."

"Reckon so, yeah."

"I never thought I'd be here with you."

"No, Jasper. Nobody does. Nobody's at home daydreaming about this kind of trip to the clinic."

"I just want to make sure this is your call. Your idea. Not me putting ideas in your head."

"In my little head."

"What?"

"The way you said that. You might as well have said 'in your little head.'"

"Your head's huge, Bea."

"Oh? Yeah? Since the—"

"The haircut, yeah. It's huge. It's enormous. How'd it ever get out the birth canal?"

"Cesarean."

"But what I actually mean is you're smart. Real smart. And I guess if I put ideas in your head you would chuck them right back out, because you're smart. And you've got a good haircut."

"All these compliments. So nice."

"No."

"No what?"

"I'm not. Not nice. I'm an asshole."

"Sure. If that makes you feel better. You're an asshole, Jasper. We are here because you're an asshole. Case closed."

"It doesn't make me feel better."

Her voice crackles angry for the first time. "Of course it does."

"How could it?"

"Self-flagellation."

"Is that when monks hit themselves in the balls?"

"Yeah. You like beating yourself up. It gets you off. I know you."

"Isn't that better than not feeling bad? Don't you want me to feel bad about it?"

"I don't care about your feelings, Jasper. I'm here for me. Not you."

"So maybe only you should do it."

"The process takes two people. That's how it knows how to rewrite shit. Perpetrator and victim, working together, hippocampuses allied."

"I thought you hated 'victim.'"

"I'm not a survivor. I didn't survive you. You're not bad enough to have to *survive*. You're just the straw that broke the camel's back. That's all. You're a straw."

"How is your back?"

"Not bad on two tabs an hour."

He pivots all the way around on his seat, one leg pulled up to his chest, so he can face her. His voice is stretched. "Remember when you needed someone to drive you to the hospital for a colonoscopy? And I did, and for the spot on the form where it said 'relation' I put 'grandma'? Then later I picked you up and you were loopy as fuck?"

"I remember."

"You wanted chicken fingers and a big blue slushie. Blue-flavored, not blueberry."

"So?"

"I'm going to see if the vending machines have anything good. You want a drink?"

"I'm good. Thanks."

He glances toward the empty service desk. "Wouldn't it be awful to have the guy look you right in the eye and recognize you and you realize you've been here before?"

He gets up and goes to the vending machine and trails his fingers over the glowing buttons. She takes three pills from a bottle in her purse. He comes back and sits down.

"The next day I didn't even remember it. It was only when you told me. Then it hit me like a fucking brick. And I thought, how? How could I do that? But I remembered."

"That's why we're here."

"I want to keep saying I'm sorry forever."

"I get that, yeah."

"But I might not be."

She blinks. "You might not be."

"You might be right about it all just being performative. Monks hitting themselves in the balls. How can I tell if I'm really sorry? Especially now that we're here."

She claws a hand across her face. "This is ridiculous. It's still about you, right? Still somehow about you."

"It's about both of us. But I only get to see out of my own eyes and brain and whatever, no matter how hard I try not to."

"Uh-huh."

"And when I lay it all out, like all the facts, I know I did something really shitty..."

"You keep saying that. You keep talking about this 'shitty thing' you did. You've never actually said what it is. Were you scared I would record it?"

"I didn't want to say what it was in case it was different from what you remembered. I didn't want to skew things by accident."

"Okay. I'll tell you what happened. We were splitting a hotel room at the conference. Because we're friends."

"We are."

"What?"

"We are friends. I mean, all the other stuff, all the good things, those are still real things."

She looks him in the eye and speaks evenly. "You climbed into my bed and hugged me and said it was nice catching up with everybody and then you pushed my head all the way down your chest to your pulled-out cock."

His flat face goes red. For a moment he's silent. "I thought I didn't do that kind of thing."

She gives a half laugh. "Thing! Thing. You thought you didn't sexually assault people."

"It wasn't that simple." He has a sly venom in his voice. "You already admitted it wasn't that simple. The second message."

"Bet you screenshotted it."

"No. Everything's gone. I used the same virus you did. With the rewrite algorithm. Our new conversation was about truffles. Like, if people still eat them."

"I saw."

"We've hooked up before."

"Before I was married, yeah."

"That night, when we went out to celebrate the book. We were flirting. You said that in the second message."

"Yeah. Yes. We had been drunkenly flirting at dinner. It wasn't supposed to go anywhere."

"And you said you touched my chest."

"Yeah. When you got into bed, I touched your chest. I was drunk."

"I was drunk. So don't call it that. Don't call it assault. Don't act like it was a crime."

"It was disgusting."

"Yeah. But you let me hang on a meathook for a whole day before you sent that second message. You let me think I did it out of nowhere."

"Boo-hoo for your bad day. I let this eat me alive for three weeks."

"I'm sorry."

"If you'd tried to kiss me or something, that would have been different. But you just grabbed me like I was a prop. Like, lucky girl, you have the correct assemblage of orifices. And people have been grabbing me like that my whole life. And it makes me want to scream."

"You can tell people. What I did was shitty. I can't make you not tell people. It's completely your right to tell people."

"I don't want to do that. I don't want to do that to my partner. Don't want to do it to myself. I don't want to be one of those brave women, okay? I don't owe brave to anybody. Unless." She pauses. "Unless I thought you were going to do it again. Or do worse. To somebody else." She looks at him. "And I don't think you will."

His gaze flickers to one side.

"Jasper?"

"Bea."

Her breath is a shudder. "You said you never expected to be here with me. Did you expect to be here with someone else?"

"Eventually." He peels the word up like a scab. "Maybe. I don't know. I wouldn't mean to."

"What does that mean, you wouldn't mean to?"

"Things happen. You party. Partied. You know what it's like. People who say it's always this clear-cut thing, this easy thing, it's like they've never been fucked up in their life, you know?"

"Why are you telling me this?"

"Because it's true. Things are messy in the dark. There's stuff I don't remember. Not because I scrubbed it, but because I was blackout. The way I grew up, small town, oil town, it was like, men do this. You're a man, so you do this. And women want that. Even if they act like they don't."

"Stop talking, Jasp. Just stop."

"I can't. This is my one chance to say it. This one time, this was middle school, we were all in the basement, and my friend's brother had a clip of this girl sucking his cock, and he was showing us. And he was telling us about these other girls, all these other girls. And he said, sometimes girls don't know exactly what they want. Sometimes you have to nudge it a little. Force it a little. And he took this big swig of beer, real solemn, and everyone nodded and drank their beers too. And I was holding it in my mouth for the longest time, the carbonation, the bubbles, all crackling and burning in my mouth, because I still hated beer. It was Heineken. And then I swallowed."

"Yeah. I get it. You swallowed. All you have to do is shut up, Jasper. Just shut up for a second, just one fucking second. I've been shutting up my whole life, and even now, even when you do this to me, you're still the one talking. Why are you still talking?"

"I'm sorry." He pauses. "It's because that's the only thing I'm good at. Is talking."

"Debatable."

"And if I never moved away, I'd still think that way. That basement way. And those people who think that way, they're not evil. They're not monsters. They're just people. Lots of them are my friends. And lots of them grew up. Some of them didn't. But they're not monsters."

"You think I don't know a hundred guys like that?"

"So you know I'm not a monster."

"What do you want from me? Seriously. What do you want from me right now, in this situation? You want me to tell you that deep down you're a good guy? Or do you want me to tell you you're an incurable asshole? Make up your fucking mind."

"I don't know. I don't know." He clamps his palms over his head, rubs his forehead with the heels of his hands. "When we gave each other signed copies of the book, the morning after. You wrote something in mine. You wrote, 'You're a good egg.'"

"That's what I write when I don't know what to write."

"You didn't know what to write? We worked on that book together for a year and a half."

"Yeah, and the night before you tried to put your cock in my mouth."

He sags. "How can I make it right? Because this, us being here, this isn't going to make it right."

She jerks up out of her seat and her bag nearly topples before she snatches it. When she speaks her voice is a snarl. "This is the *only way* it will be right."

"It's like running away."

"I know what you want. I've got it figured out, even if you haven't yet. You want to be crucified and exonerated at the same fucking time. You want people to tell you you're a miserable excuse for a human, and then marvel at how sensitive you are for realizing it. That doesn't happen. It never will."

"Look. You shouldn't have to live with it. I should."

"You think I'm getting it scrubbed because I can't handle the trauma? I told you, Jasper. You're a straw. I'm getting it scrubbed because we work well together. We have another translation contract in June. And because, yes, when you're not being self-pitying and shitty, you're fun to drink with. You're even dependable in the drive-you-to-a-colonoscopy way. And I've put too much time into you to cut you out of my life." She sets her bag on the empty seat beside her. "Even if there was a way I could scrub it without you, we'd never have that back. You'd always be acting. Eventually it would slip. I'd know something was wrong. We'd drift apart. Be uneasy for months. Years. Then you'd call me up drunk one night and confess, and we'd be back to square one, wouldn't we?"

He doesn't reply. A cleaner wanders into the room on spidery plastic legs. It secretes a bright blue detergent onto the floor.

"If I don't remember it, I won't learn from it."

She sits back down. "I'm not your teacher. If you didn't know it was wrong without me telling you, you'll never know. You'll always just be going through the motions."

"Maybe that's the trick, then. Is just going through the motions." His face is his idea of grave. "But I know myself too well, Bea. To say I'll never end up in that kind of situation again."

"Maybe stop fucking drinking."

"Are you going to stop drinking?"

"No."

They watch the cleaner work, circular brushes whirring and whipping the detergent into pale blue foam.

He inhales. "Okay. Here's what it is. I tried to put your mouth on my cock. I made you feel like a prop. It was a shitty thing to do. All I was thinking, the only thing I was thinking, was that it would feel good for me. And you not wanting it didn't even enter my brain. Maybe because of old memories. Maybe because I was wasted. I can say there's no excuse, but I've always got more of them."

She shakes her head. "Here's what it is. In the big picture, you're nothing. What you did was nothing. But in the little picture, it sucked. Because I didn't think you would do something like that, and now I know you would. And I felt disgusted and disappointed and disrespected. And angry. I wanted to cut your dick off."

"Yeah. Yeah." His eyes are already lightening. "But I'm not a bad person. Or a good person. I'm just a person who does things that make people either happy or unhappy. Usually I do the happy kind. This time I did the unhappy kind."

"Moral philosophy for toddlers."

"If there's nothing I can do to fix it, and if I'm not planning to do it again, then this was the best option. Coming here. You were right."

"Yeah. I was." She shuts her eyes. "I'm exhausted. I'm fucking exhausted and I don't want to hate anyone or teach anyone or love anyone despite their bullshit. I just want it to be gone."

"Gone. Yeah."

The memory technician comes out, clutching a tablet in gloved hands. "Sorry about that wait, folks. Calibration's finished. Integrated deletion for Jasper and Beatrice?"

"Yeah." He takes a deep breath and stands up. "Here we go. I'm glad. I'm really glad. I value you a lot, you know, Bea?"

She stands up and walks with him down the antiseptic-smelling hallway. She doesn't look the technician in the face. She knows better.

■

Rich Larson was born in Galmi, Niger, has studied in Rhode Island and worked in the south of Spain, and now lives in Ottawa, Canada. He is the author of Annex *and* Cypher, *as well as over a hundred short stories— some of the best of which can be found in his collection* Tomorrow Factory. *His work has been translated into Polish, Czech, French, Italian, Vietnamese and Chinese. Besides writing, he enjoys traveling, learning languages, playing soccer, watching basketball, shooting pool, and dancing kizomba.*

ON EARTH AS IT IS IN HEAVEN

■

Horacio Quiroz

Based in México City. After working for several years in the advertising industry, I began my self-taught painting studies in 2013.

I graduated in Graphic Design from Universidad Iberoamericana, following this I worked for nearly twelve years as a Creative Art Director for various renowned international advertising agencies, such as Publicis México and Zeta Advertising. During this time I took care of accounts such as Coca-Cola, VW, BMW, Maytag, Nido, Garnier, The Home Depot, Gerber and many others. As a publicist I learned to work under pressure on several projects at once. I gained a thorough understanding of how the industry works through dealing with customers, planners, brand managers, designers, producers, models etc.

Despite working full time as a publicist, my artistic education never stopped as I was always learning from the work of other art directors and great photographers, who I was fortunate to work with both here in Mexico and abroad.

In 2013, driven by my passion for the visual arts, I decided to leave advertising and devote myself entirely to artistic activity with a goal of reconnecting with the spontaneity I had in my childhood. Thus, over the last six years I have launched myself on a new career path, experimenting with various self-taught techniques of pictorial representation, formats and themes, which have guided how I define my vision and identity as an artist. This change in my life has given rise to deep personal introspection, closely linked to what now shapes my body of work.

Printed in the USA
CPSIA information can be obtained
at www.ICGtesting.com
LVHW041029130823
755062LV00032B/216